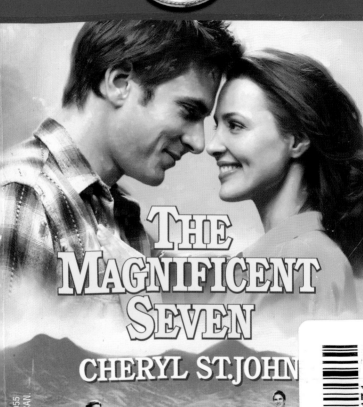

THE MAGNIFICENT SEVEN

CHERYL ST.JOHN

SILHOUETTE · 65055
$4.50 U.S./$5.25 CAN.

MONTANA MAVERICKS:
WED IN WHITEHORN—

12 BRAND-NEW stories where legends live on and love lasts forever!

On sale...

ISBN 0-373-65055-8

Only from

Silhouette®
Where love comes alive™

*Available wherever
Silhouette books are sold.*

Visit Silhouette at www.eHarlequin.com
PSMONMIFC

What had just happened to her?

More than once, Heather had found herself looking at Mitch Fielding with preposterously sexy thoughts. She'd never mused in that feverish manner before.

Remembering the way Mitch's simple touch set her skin tingling, she closed her eyes and relished the memories. The strength of her reactions frightened her. Looking at him, smelling him… Heather's chest fluttered.

She was the almost-thirty-year-old mother of three children. She'd been married. And she'd never had these overpowering feelings toward a man before.

Her body remembered his touch. His kiss. The intoxicating loss of control and the frantic desire to possess, be possessed. The lack of restraint terrified her.

And thrilled her.

The question was, how much courage did she really possess?

MONTANA MAVERICKS: WED IN WHITEHORN
Brand-new stories beneath the Big Sky!

MONTANA MAVERICKS

CHERYL ST.JOHN

is the pseudonym for Nebraska author Cheryl Ludwigs. Cheryl's first book. *Rain Shadow*, received nominations for awards from *Romantic Times Magazine* and *Affaire de Coeur* and for the Romance Writers of America's RITA Award. Her Silhouete Intimate Moments title *The Truth about Toby* won a reader award from the Wisconsin RWA's "Write Touch" contest.

Cheryl has served her Heartland RWA chapter as president, vice president, program director, Published Author's Network liaison and conference committee chairman.

A married mother of four and a grandmother several times over, Cheryl enjoys her family. In her "spare" time, she corresponds with writers and readers, and she would love to hear from you.

Send a SASE to: P.O. Box 12142, Florence Station, Omaha, NE 68112-0142.

MONTANA MAVERICKS

THE MAGNIFICENT SEVEN

CHERYL ST.JOHN

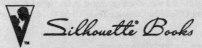

Published by Silhouette Books
America's Publisher of Contemporary Romance

If you purchased this book without a cover you should be aware that this book is stolen property. It was reported as "unsold and destroyed" to the publisher, and neither the author nor the publisher has received any payment for this "stripped book."

Special thanks and acknowledgment are given to Cheryl St.John for her contribution to the MONTANA MAVERICKS: WED IN WHITEHORN series.

 SILHOUETTE BOOKS

ISBN 0-373-65055-8

THE MAGNIFICENT SEVEN

Copyright © 2000 by Harlequin Books S.A.

All rights reserved. Except for use in any review, the reproduction or utilization of this work in whole or in part in any form by any electronic, mechanical or other means, now known or hereafter invented, including xerography, photocopying and recording, or in any information storage or retrieval system, is forbidden without the written permission of the editorial office, Silhouette Books, 300 East 42nd Street, New York, NY 10017 U.S.A.

All characters in this book have no existence outside the imagination of the author and have no relation whatsoever to anyone bearing the same name or names. They are not even distantly inspired by any individual known or unknown to the author, and all incidents are pure invention.

This edition published by arrangement with Harlequin Books S.A.

® and TM are trademarks of Harlequin Books S.A., used under license. Trademarks indicated with ® are registered in the United States Patent and Trademark Office, the Canadian Trade Marks Office and in other countries.

Visit Silhouette at www.eHarlequin.com

Printed in U.S.A.

MONTANA MAVERICKS

Wed in Whitehorn

Welcome to Whitehorn, Montana—
a place of passion and adventure.
Seems this charming little town has some
Big Sky secrets. And everybody's talking about…

Heather Johnson: She'd vowed never to return to Whitehorn. But her father's death and an inherited ranch prompted a temporary sojourn, three kids in tow, to sell her childhood home. Yet the anticipated "fix-up" was an overhaul that required carpenter Mitch Fielding's expert touch.

Mitch Fielding: Mitch bargained with the beautiful single mom: He'd do repairs for reduced pay…*if* she baby-sat his twins. It was hard work raising his little girls, harder still knowing he'd uprooted them to meet the mighty Kincaids, his secret father's family. Hardest of all was knowing Heather intended to leave, no matter how magnificent their life together could be.…

Collin Kincaid and **Hope Baxter:** Though the long-standing battle between their families had just been reignited, nothing could stop the sparks that flew when the Kincaid heir came face-to-face with Baxter's beautiful daughter.…

Audra Westwood: Gavin Nighthawk's murder charge made Audra gloat…until the news broke that powerful Garrett Kincaid was financing Nighthawk's defense.…

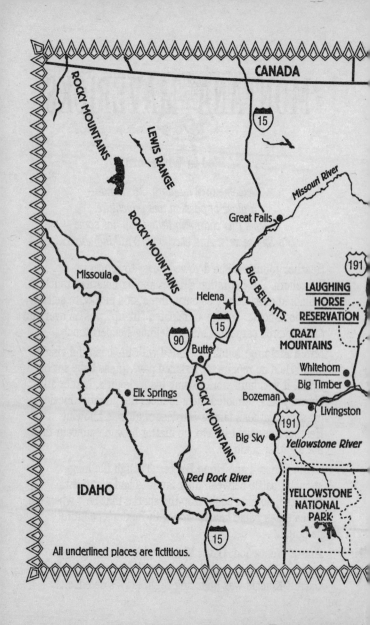

CANADA

ROCKY MOUNTAINS

LEWIS RANGE

ROCKY MOUNTAINS

15

Missouri River

Great Falls

Missoula

BIG BELT MTS.

Helena

191

LAUGHING HORSE RESERVATION

CRAZY MOUNTAINS

15

90

Butte

ROCKY MOUNTAINS

Whitehorn

Big Timber

Elk Springs

Bozeman

Livingston

191

Big Sky

Yellowstone River

Red Rock River

IDAHO

YELLOWSTONE NATIONAL PARK

15

All underlined places are fictitious.

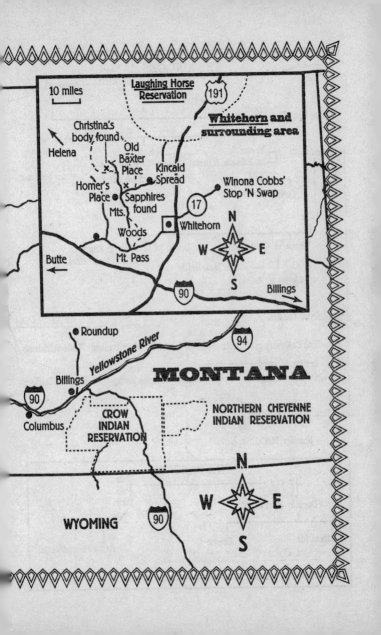

MONTANA MAVERICKS: WED IN WHITEHORN
THE KINCAIDS

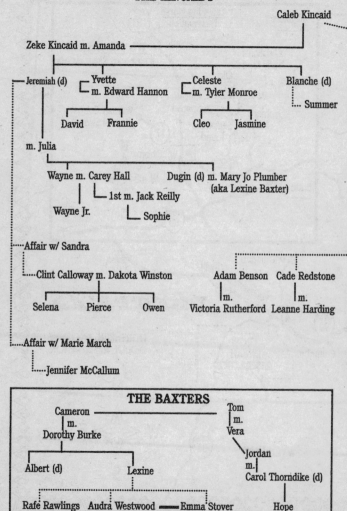

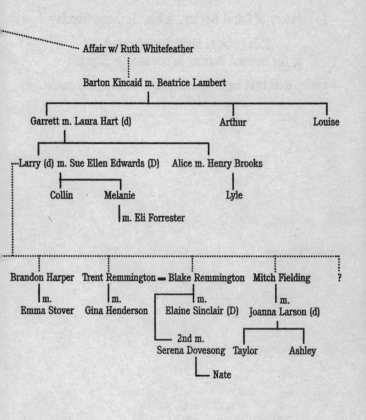

Affair w/ Ruth Whitefeather

Barton Kincaid m. Beatrice Lambert

Garrett m. Laura Hart (d)   Arthur   Louise

Larry (d) m. Sue Ellen Edwards (D)   Alice m. Henry Brooks

Collin   Melanie   Lyle

m. Eli Forrester

Brandon Harper   Trent Remmington — Blake Remmington   Mitch Fielding   ?

m.   m.   m.   m.

Emma Stover   Gina Henderson   Elaine Sinclair (D)   Joanna Larson (d)

2nd m.

Serena Dovesong   Taylor   Ashley

Nate

Symbols
..... Child of an Affair
— Twins
d   Deceased
D   Divorced

In memory of Carol Backus, a.k.a. Suzanne Barclay

This book is lovingly dedicated
to the newest darling in our family: Elijah.

I praise God that he is fearfully and wonderfully made.

One

Mitch Fielding led his twin six-year-olds, Taylor and Ashley, through the lunch crowd at the Hip Hop Café as though he were guiding them through a minefield. Taylor narrowly missed knocking over a gray-haired gent's cane that was leaning against a table edge, and Mitch clamped his hand firmly over Ashley's mouth as soon as he noticed an overweight woman shoveling chocolate-cream pie between her lips.

He got them settled into a booth and released his breath. "There." He picked up the plastic-coated menu and scanned for something nourishing the twins would eat without pitching a fit. "They have hamburgers and chicken fingers."

"Yuck. I want a chocolate malt and a pickle," Ashley pronounced.

"I want skettios," Taylor said.

"They don't have skettios," he replied to one daughter, then turned to the other. "And you can have a chocolate malt if you eat a hamburger."

"Gross. I don't want a hamburger." She folded her arms over the front of her Teletubbie T-shirt. "I want a pickle."

"You can have a pickle with your hamburger. Taylor, they have spaghetti."

"Don't like spaghetti."

"Of course you do. It's the same stuff that comes out of the cans, only real."

"Uh-uh-uh," she said in a singsongy voice with a shake of her head. "It doesn't taste the same."

He resisted the urge to argue or bargain in public, which always made him feel as if his daughters were getting the upper hand anyway. How long could a child survive on pickles, malts and canned spaghetti? It was his job as a parent to see that they were well nourished, but how did he go about it? Some nights he dropped into bed mentally exhausted, feeling lucky to have gotten several bites of anything into them.

A waitress appeared at his elbow, and Mitch glanced up to see the slim blonde in a blue T-shirt proclaiming Breakfast Served All Day give him a curious once-over. Everyone in Whitehorn, Montana, seemed to know each other, and he obviously stuck out as a newcomer. A quick scan confirmed that a dozen eyes had zeroed in on him and his daughters.

"Afternoon," she said pleasantly. "I'm Janie Austin. Which one of Garrett Kincaid's grandsons are you?"

"Mitch Fielding," he replied self-consciously. "How did you know?"

She cast him a friendly smile. "In Whitehorn everybody knows everybody else's business. Anticipating each grandson's arrival has been the hot topic for quite a while.''

He didn't know how well he liked being the subject of gossip, but this young woman seemed friendly and accepting enough. Apparently everyone already knew he was one of six illegitimate grandsons the old man had summoned to his ranch. Garrett was still searching for a seventh.

She touched his shoulder in a brief gesture of greeting that put him at ease. ''Nice to meet you, Mitch.''

He returned her neighborly smile. ''These are my daughters, Taylor and Ashley.''

''Look at that pretty blond hair. What'll you have, girls?''

He gave her their orders, amid objections from his daughters. Taylor waved her arm to get his attention and knocked the ketchup bottle into the salt and pepper shakers. Pepper spilled on the laminate tabletop, and she promptly blew it into her sister's face.

Ashley sneezed and her eyes watered. She grabbed for the rolled paper napkin that held her silverware and sent the metal utensils flying across the table and onto the floor.

Mitch picked up the utensils, handed them to the astonished waitress and admonished the girls to sit on their behinds.

By the time their food arrived, everyone in the room knew Taylor had to go to the bathroom. He took them to the women's room, standing outside until their food was cold. Finally he rapped on the door.

Thank God it was a one-seater, because he had to go in to dry their hands and pull them out. So that the next person wouldn't slip and break her neck, he mentioned to the waitress that the rest room floor was flooded.

"My spaghetti's cold," Taylor complained loudly.

"So's everything else." With a sigh, Mitch picked up his cold burger and took a bite, just as Ashley knocked over her malt.

Twenty minutes later he released their hands to get his wallet and pay the cashier. He ran back to leave a generous tip at the table for the patient waitress.

A bulletin board on the wall by the cash register caught his attention and, ignoring the yanks on his hands, he scanned the notices of cars and household items for sale. He was particularly looking for someone to watch the girls for him so he could line up a few jobs. Most of the Want Ads had been placed by junior and high school students; the twins needed someone more experienced. Much more experienced. A warden, perhaps.

One notice caught his eye. Handyman Wanted. He released a small hand to tap the card with his forefinger.

"Know anything about this one?" He directed his question to the gray-haired waitress in orthopedic shoes standing near the cash register.

"That's Pete Bolton's ranch," she replied. "His daughter was in here a couple of weeks ago, looking for someone to help her fix up the place to sell."

That sounded like just the job for him. A couple of months back he'd had to sell all of his contracts, to take care of the girls. His mother had been caring for them, but one calamity after another had pulled him from work sites, until it wasn't fair to his customers or his subcontractors for him to continue. While trying to figure out what to do, he'd decided that Garrett Kincaid's invitation was just the solution.

This had been the perfect time to do some traveling, and he'd been eager to spend more time with, and get to know, this grandfather he'd never known existed until last May.

"Do you have some paper I can write the number on?" he asked.

"Sure, sugar." She fished in her pocket, came out with her order tablet and a pen, and scribbled the phone number, tearing off the sheet and handing it to him.

The bell over the door clanged and he turned to see one of his daughters dash outside.

"Thanks." He stuffed the paper into his shirt pocket and pulled the other child out the door behind him.

Lily Mae Wheeler got up out of her permanent seat in the first booth and walked over to Charlene, her gaudy jewelry clanking at her wrists and weighing down her bony chest.

"Heard he was at Garrett's ranch," she said to let Charlene know she'd been the first to hear. "Nobody knows much about him yet, 'cept his wife died when those two were just babies. Those children are holy terrors, have you ever seen the likes?''

"Must be difficult for a young father to raise two girls alone," Janie said sympathetically, coming up beside them.

"They need a good paddling, if you ask me," Lily Mae scoffed.

"Be interesting to see what happens at the Bolton ranch this afternoon, wouldn't it?" Charlene said with a devilish smile.

The three exchanged amused glances.

Engaging her ten-year-old daughter's help, Heather Johnson tackled the stack of dishes from lunch and breakfast.

"We need a dishwasher, Mom." Jessica dried a chipped plate and stood on tiptoe to place it in the cupboard.

"I didn't think we were going to be here long enough to need one," Heather replied with a regretful sigh. She turned and glanced at her sons who sat on the worn linoleum floor with coloring books. With his tongue angled out the side of his mouth, five-year-old Patrick studiously labored to keep the purple crayon inside the lines on the page. Two-year-old Andrew spent more time chasing the crayons under the table and tasting them than he did coloring, but at least her boys were temporarily occupied.

When she'd brought her children to the ranch after her father's death, she'd planned to take a two-week vacation, go through her father's personal belongings, and sell the property. A neat-and-tidy plan, something that should have gone smoothly.

Now, two and a half weeks later, she still hadn't been able to make any progress on selling. She hadn't planned on all the repairs that the real estate lady had suggested be made to get a decent price. Heather hadn't been back to Whitehorn in years, and the property had deteriorated more than she'd imagined. Her father obviously hadn't paid any more attention to the house than he ever had to her.

She shrugged off the depressing thought and gave Jessica a smile. "Thank you, angel. You are a big help to me, you know that?"

Wiping another plate, her daughter nodded in a grown-up manner. "Can we do something fun after this, Mom?"

A little pang of regret snagged Heather. She knew it hadn't been much fun for Jess to help with the boys all morning while Heather went through boxes and trunks and years' worth of accumulated junk. "What would you like to do?"

"Catch turtles in the pond?"

Heather wrinkled her nose. "Who's going to wade out there with the net?"

"You'll help, won't you?"

Heather had to admit she'd been appreciating this much-needed time with her kids. She loved her public relations job in San Francisco, and the sense of self-worth it had always brought, but she often felt guilty

about the time she missed with her children. This time
with them had been enjoyable, even though it had to
be spent here—the last place on earth she'd choose
to vacation.

She tapped Jessica on the nose with a sudsy finger.
"Okay, I'll help you catch a turtle."

Jessica grinned that knockout smile, revealing dim-
ples that would one day drive young men crazy.
Heather's heart gave a sad twinge at the thought. She
wasn't too concerned about her daughter's future.
She'd tried her best to ensure Jessica wouldn't make
the same mistakes Heather had made.

Patrick jumped up and ran to the screen door that
overlooked the long gravel drive. "Somebody's coming! It's a way cool truck!"

Andrew got up, crunching crayons beneath his red-
and-blue tennis shoes in the process, and followed his
brother. "Thumbody coming!" he mimicked.

Heather dried her hands and moved to the door.
She'd been expecting the man who had called earlier
about interviewing for the handyman job. The blue-
and-silver duel cab Silverado pickup leaving a dust
trail must belong to him.

"This is the appointment I was expecting." She
hung up the towel. "We'll be discussing business in
the other room. I want all of you to play quietly in
here until we're finished."

She waited for the children's nods of understanding, then stepped back to the door.

The driver parked in the gravel area behind the

house, but instead of getting out right away he turned toward the back seat. Heather noticed a couple of heads she hadn't seen at first. He'd brought *children* to a job interview? One big strike against him.

She stepped out onto the back porch, the age-splintered boards creaking precariously beneath her feet.

He exited the truck at last, closing the door and glancing over his shoulder.

He was tall, she noticed right away. Maybe thirty, with sandy-brown hair and a golden tan attesting to hours working in the sun.

The jeans he wore encased long legs and slim hips. A navy-blue, button-down knit shirt, work boots, and a slim black folder with a clipboard completed the classically sexy look of a handyman. Heather could picture him with a tool belt around his hips and smiled to herself. Certainly nothing wrong with his appearance.

He neared the porch. "Mrs. Johnson?"

She composed her face and nodded.

"Mitch Fielding."

She reached to shake his hand. He had calluses on his palms. Hardworking. Steadfast. *Where had that come from?* It had been a long time since she'd noticed a man the way she noticed this one. Perturbed, she released his hand. "We can talk inside."

He glanced uncomfortably over his shoulder.

"Your children?" she asked.

He nodded. "They're supposed to sit there until I get back."

She wondered again why he'd brought them along. It was completely unprofessional. "Would you like to let them come in and color at the kitchen table?"

"No," he said immediately with a shake of his head. "I don't think so."

She glanced at the truck, seeing he'd left the windows partially down. It wasn't a hot day and this meeting shouldn't take more than a few minutes. The children would be safe.

She led the way through the kitchen, reminding her own to play quietly until she was finished with her business.

"Your kids?" he asked, turning his head to observe the trio at the table.

She nodded.

They entered the sparsely furnished room her father had used for an office. Pushing aside a drawer she'd been emptying, she sat in the cracked leather chair and Mitch took the wooden one.

"Sorry about your father," he said, catching her off guard.

She fumbled with her thoughts for a moment before realizing he meant Pete Bolton's recent death. "Thank you. I came here nearly three weeks ago to sort through things and sell the ranch, but the house and outbuildings are in terrible condition, as you've seen. The Realtor wants me to fix up the property. She suggested updating the house, but I don't know if I want to go to that much trouble and expense, and I don't know the first thing about how to go about it.''

''I'm a contractor,'' he said. ''That's what I do for a living. You could leave all that up to me.''

''I didn't see you in the directory.''

''I'm not from Whitehorn. I'm here visiting my grandfather.'' When she didn't comment, he opened the folder he'd brought and presented her with several sheets of paper. ''These are my references and specs on similar projects.''

Heather glanced through the impressive details, not questioning his ability. ''I don't have funds for a big undertaking.''

He nodded understandingly. ''I don't require a retainer. You wouldn't have to pay me until you've seen the work in progress. Sometimes I can get suppliers to delay billing until after the sale goes through. I could work on that. If not, I'll handle the cost until the place is sold.''

That sounded encouraging. Still, there was the eventual expense of his fee, which would be considerable, with all the hours needed to get the place in shape. Remodeling would be ideal and bring the best price, but a quick fix was about all she could afford.

He glanced at the desk and back up. ''Are you home all day long?''

She nodded, wondering why he'd asked. Did he think her children would get in the way of construction projects? ''Unless I go into town to shop.''

"I might have a solution for both of us."

She'd been studying the papers, but she glanced up, caught off guard by the way the navy shirt sculpted his solid-looking chest and arms. She focused deliberately on his face. His disturbingly sensual lips pursed for a moment, then opened as he spoke. The odd little tremor in her stomach must have been caused by too much coffee that morning.

"Maybe we can work something out. I've been trying to find someone to keep my girls for me, so I can work. I would lower my bid considerably in exchange for you taking care of them while I do the job."

Heather dragged her distracted thoughts from his arresting appearance and mulled his suggestion over. It did sound like a wise arrangement. And she was here anyway.

Childish shrieks caught their attention at the same time. Heather listened, but Mitch immediately jumped off his seat and shot out of the room, surprising her with his agility. She followed.

Her three children had gathered at the screen door to see what was going on outside. They gave Mitch wide berth as he bolted past, then followed Heather out onto the porch.

The shiny Silverado, which had been parked on the gravel behind the house only minutes ago, now rolled slowly toward the corner of the corral, gaining momentum.

Heather watched in horror. Her gaze immediately searched for whoever had been in the back seat.

Thank goodness, two blond-haired girls stood on the grass, clinging to each other, jumping and screaming as the truck crunched into the wooden coral fence, flattened the corner sections with a crack, and kept going.

Mitch had reached the girls, checked them over for injuries, then ran after his truck, which was now on the grassy slope leading to the pond. Heather followed in dismay. The screen door slammed forgotten behind her.

By the time she reached the edge of the pond, the pickup had come to a stop, the entire front end submerged in the green water, the tailgate pointing toward the horizon.

Two

Mitch Fielding stood on the bank and sank the fingers of one hand into his hair in frustration. He splayed the other hand on his hip.

Heather came up behind him in time to hear the curt expletive whistled from between his rigid lips. He turned quickly. "Sorry."

She absently waved his apology away. They both turned and gaped at his partially submerged truck. Behind them, the girls continued to howl shrill cries of terror.

A little anxious over what this stranger's reaction might be, Heather glanced at his profile. He stared in disbelief, and she couldn't help feeling sorry for him.

"You think it'll sink more?" a childish voice asked.

Heather turned to see that her own kids had followed and now stood beside them. Patrick had asked the question and gazed wide-eyed up at Mitch. Heather readied herself to hush him or move her children safely back.

Mitch studied the situation and replied calmly, "I don't think so. Probably hit a rock or something that's holding it there.'' He turned to Heather. ''You have a truck or a tractor?''

''There are both in the machine shed,'' she answered with relief at his composed reaction. ''I'll get you the keys.'' Taking a few steps, she turned back. ''Need some help?''

''I need some help, all right,'' he muttered, following her up the incline.

Mitch couldn't believe this had happened. He'd had a perfect chance at a job; now this woman would never hire him. As he neared the girls, Ashley gaped at him with wide blue eyes, her tears subsiding. Taylor threw herself on the ground and wailed.

''Which one of you did this?'' he asked.

''I told her you'd be real mad,'' Ashley said. ''I told her we should stay strapped in just like you said.''

''No, you din't!'' Taylor whined, halting her histrionics long enough to sit up and argue. ''You took your seat belt off first!''

''How did that truck move?'' he demanded to know. ''I had the engine turned off and the key with me.'' He stuck his hand in his pocket and pulled out his key ring, dangling it in front of them, but assuring himself. There was no way he would have left the key in the ignition, and the gearshift wouldn't budge without the key.

''Taylor got the 'mergency key. I told her not to.''

''No, you din't! You said maybe we could drive back home!''

He groaned. He'd had a magnetic holder under the front fender, with an extra ignition key, in case he ever locked himself out. But he hadn't figured they'd known it was there. He should have known better than to underestimate their uncanny ability to find something they shouldn't and wreak havoc. "How did you know that key was there?" he asked, bewildered.

"You took it out and gave it to the man who fixed the horn. That day we got a borrowed truck."

Sure enough, he had. And they'd seen him do it. How careless of him. But he'd never imagined—

"Here." Heather Johnson had returned from a trek into her house and dangled a key ring out in front of him. "I really don't know what's what on here, but I think that's the tractor key there. I'm not sure how it runs or if there's gas in the tank. If not, there's a pump beside the barn."

"Thanks." He looked down at his daughters, lost for a suitable punishment, stunned by his own incompetence. Sometimes life was just so overwhelming, he didn't know which way to turn.

"I'll keep an eye on them," the unsuspecting woman said kindly.

Mitch cast his daughters a look that would blister paint and bent over them to ensure intimidation. "You be quiet and *nice* until I get my truck out of the water. Then I'll deal with you."

Four watery blue eyes riveted on his face and two identical chins quivered. The girls nodded solemnly.

He located the tractor, an amazingly well-kept old

Alice Chalmers that would probably bring a small fortune at an antique auction, checked it for gas, and lifted a tow chain down from the wall.

He drove the smooth-running tractor to the pond and waded out to the Silverado, lamenting his beautiful cab filled with scummy water. Noting that the gearshift was in Neutral, he made his way back to dry ground.

Hooking the chain to the truck axle, he climbed onto the seat and slowly eased the tractor forward, pulling the truck out. Murky green water streamed all the way up the incline. He stopped the tractor in the gravel parking area and got down to secure the pickup. Water dripped from beneath the hood and from the bottoms of the doors. A long crease marred the front fender where it had scraped along the fence post. He'd sure been fond of this truck.

He opened the driver's door and a gush of water hit his already soaked boots. He glanced around and found the girls sitting on the porch with the Johnsons, the entire group watching the proceedings with apprehensive interest.

He placed the gearshift in Park and opened the other door, though not hopeful of the interior drying out anytime soon. At least Taylor and Ashley were all right. That was what was important, he told himself, gritting his teeth. It was, after all, just a truck. A very *expensive* truck.

Heather Johnson and the children walked toward him. She'd picked up her youngest and carried him on her hip. Her eyes held a mixture of apprehension and curiosity, and for some reason he didn't care for the fact that she was a little bit afraid of him.

"You gonna keep that turtle, mister?" The oldest child questioned him with wide hazel eyes, eyes very different from her mother's.

Mitch followed her gaze and discovered the turtle that had been swept out of his cab on that last rush of pond water. The creature had poked head and feet out of its shell and was lumbering slowly toward the grass. "No."

"Hey, look, Mama!" she said, hurrying over to kneel near the animal, who stopped and tucked its head into the shell. "You won't have to find us a turtle now! The man caught us this one. Thanks!"

The rest of the kids gathered around the turtle and touched its shell.

"No problem." He raised his gaze to the woman's and found her studying him with those golden-brown eyes that still revealed a hint of mistrust. "Sorry about our interview. And about—" he glanced around and felt tingling heat climb into his cheeks "—*this*. I'll fix your corral right away."

"How long do you suppose it will take for your truck to dry out?" she asked.

No doubt she wondered how soon she could be rid of him. He didn't blame her. "At least a day—just to see if it will start."

The seats and carpet would never look—or smell—

the same. Wondering if his insurance would cover this, his shook his head.

"I'll give you a ride back to Whitehorn," she offered, at once very businesslike.

"I don't want to get your car wet or dirty," he said, gesturing at his soaked jeans and boots.

"I'm sure I can find you something of my father's to wear home." Apparently his actions had satisfied her fears, and he appreciated her consideration.

"I'm hungry," Taylor said.

His anger simmered anew at her words. She hadn't eaten three bites of her meal at the café. "You can wait."

"No, I can't. I'm starving!"

Embarrassed, he moved toward her.

"Why don't I fix everyone a snack while you're changing?" Heather's no-nonsense voice stopped him. He glanced over and found those disturbing eyes on him. "You can shower if you'd like. The upstairs bathroom has ancient plumbing and one of those old cast-iron tubs, but it gets the job done."

He took a calming breath. His jeans were cold and clammy and getting out of them sounded too good to pass up. "She probably won't eat anything. They're both picky eaters."

"Well, I'll see if I can't find them something." She ushered the throng toward the house, brought Mitch clothes and a towel, and directed him to the upstairs bathroom. He couldn't help watching her walk away, her denim shorts a mere teasing cover-up for a softly rounded backside. Once she'd disappeared down the hallway, he discovered a pair of faded boxers tucked between the folded jeans and shirt.

She'd been right. The fixtures were old and the room outdated, but it was an enormous space, with a window overlooking open pastureland. He imagined the room with a Jacuzzi tub and a skylight. What he'd seen of the house so far was sound and spacious, merely sadly outdated. It would make a good family home for a relatively small investment.

Showering in the old tub, he found himself wondering how much land went with the house. Garrett wanted to give him a section of the Kincaid ranch, but right now the details were hung up in court. If Mitch had the money and the inclination to stay in Montana, this would be a good spread to look into.

Heather's father had been as tall as Mitch, but wider, so the jeans hung precariously on his hips. He wrapped his wet clothing in the towel he'd used and carried them down to the kitchen.

"I'll wash those and you can get them when you come back for your truck," Heather said, reaching for the bundle.

"No, you don't—"

"Don't argue," she insisted. "A few more things won't make a dent in the amount of laundry I do."

"Well, thank you." He released the bundle, but not his grip on his waistband.

"Here." She fished in a drawer and came up with a length of twine.

Mitch thanked her and tied the cord through the belt loops, then glanced toward the kids.

Taylor and Ashley sat at the round oak table with her children, nearly empty plates in front of them.

"We never got around to proper introductions," Heather said. "This is my daughter, Jessica, and these are my sons, Patrick and Andrew. Children, this is Mr. Fielding."

"Mitch, please," he corrected, appreciating her cordiality. She had every right to think him the biggest loser in history. Times like this, he would agree. "And you met Taylor and Ashley."

Heather nodded.

Had she ever. "They ate something?"

"Just a small snack. Grapes and raisins and a few cubes of cheese with crackers, nothing to spoil their dinner."

Spoil their dinner? As if! He marveled at the concept of them eating the nourishing fare she'd provided. The food she described was more than they ever ate for dinner! How had she done it? He wanted to ask, but he didn't want to appear even more incapable in her eyes.

"Children, wash your hands and use the bathroom. I'm going to get the Blazer." She opened a cupboard and took out a small purse.

Her children obediently carried their plates to the counter and washed their hands at the sink. Jessica pulled out a chair and helped Andrew. Mitch watched in awe.

The twins miraculously fell in behind and washed their hands without a complaint, then took their turns in the bathroom. They were still in shock over the truck incident, waiting to see what horrible punishment was going to befall them, otherwise they'd have been their usual contrary selves.

He would enjoy this compliance while it lasted, he decided, and followed the children out to the Blazer Heather had pulled up to the back porch. She got out and locked up the house, checked all the riders for seat belts, then returned to the driver's seat. Her delicate scent, something fresh and feminine, drifted toward him, and once again those disturbing eyes touched his face. This time her gaze was like a breezy caress that fingered across his brow, along his jaw.

His imagination had gone into overdrive. He looked away, and she changed gears.

"I appreciate this," Mitch said, though she really hadn't had much choice once he'd been stranded in her backyard. Get them to town or have them on her steps, he guessed.

She drove toward the county road.

"About the job..." he dared.

"I don't think that's going to work out," she replied, firmly crushing any scrawny hope he'd held.

"I had a great idea for that upstairs bath," he said, anyway. "Of course you need one downstairs, too." He explained his concept of the bath he'd envisioned. "If you change your mind, I'll be glad to work out the details with you. Like I said, I can delay payment, and I know I could keep costs down.''

"Thanks," she said, not giving him any encouragement. "I'll keep that in mind. Where am I taking you, anyway?''

"The Kincaid ranch," he replied. "Know where it is?''

"You'll have to point the way.''

He nodded. "I suppose you've heard all about the grandson roundup.''

"No.''

"Garrett Kincaid is my grandfather.'' He studied her profile, then let his attention drift to those shapely legs.

She glanced over and caught him looking. King of Cool here, he scoffed at himself. "I've only been here two and a half weeks. I live in San Francisco. I don't plan on sticking around, and I don't really know anyone in town anymore.''

He'd grown used to everyone knowing his business, so the fact that she hadn't heard all the local gossip was refreshing. For some weird reason, he found himself wanting to tell her his side of the story. "My mother is from here," he explained. "I grew up thinking I had no family on my father's side. Hearing from Garrett last year was a surprise. My biological father was Garrett's son, Larry. When he died, he left quite a few descendents—to my grandfather's surprise. Seven of us, to be exact.''

"Wow.''

"Wow is right." He kept his voice low. "He was married when he had an affair with the nanny—my mother. Apparently Larry gave her money for an abortion, but she kept it and moved to Minnesota. She told me she sent him a photo and a letter after I was born, but he never responded, so she went on with her life. Married my stepdad, had more kids."

"You don't sound upset or bitter."

"People do what they have to do. My mom did the best she knew how. My grandfather never knew about me—about any of Larry's illegitimate children—but once he found out, he did what he thought was right. Well, six of us, anyway. He's still looking for the seventh. He got us all together and is working to give us each a piece of Kincaid land."

"He sounds like a nice man."

"He is."

"And Larry?" She cast Mitch a inquisitive glance.

"What about him?"

"How do you feel about him?"

A personal question. One he hadn't anticipated from her, but he didn't mind. Her curiosity hinted that she may think a little more kindly of him than he'd worried. "I don't really know how to feel. He never wanted to be a part of my life, and I've had a fine life without him."

Heather turned onto the long strip of road that led across the Kincaid ranch to the house. "This it?"

"This is it."

"Is there a Mr. Johnson?" Mitch asked. He'd told

her quite a bit about himself, but knew nothing about her.

She cast him a quick, unrevealing glance before returning her attention to the road. "There is, but we're divorced."

"Oh."

A minute later, a quiet, "You, too?"

"No. My wife died."

"I'm sorry."

He gazed at the house that came into view ahead. "Me, too."

"Recently?" she asked.

He turned to look at her. "Four years ago. She had a blood disease."

Her eyes held compassion when she took them from the road for a moment. "So you've been raising Taylor and Ashley by yourself?"

"My mother and my wife's mother kept them, and we tried a few day cares. Nothing worked out. They're, uh, a handful."

"Most kids are."

She didn't have a clue. He'd seen how well behaved hers were. Sometimes he felt like a total failure at parenting. Heck, most times he *was* a total failure at parenting.

Well, being raised by grandmothers would explain some of the twins's spoiled behavior, Heather thought. But she'd never seen anything like their kicking and screaming histrionics, and she knew she wouldn't have put up with it for five minutes.

She pulled the Blazer up the winding drive, past detached garages, and stopped in front of the house. A tall, dark-haired young man with dark eyes and olive skin approached the vehicle, a smile on his handsome face. "Hey, bro! Where's your truck?"

"Hey, Cade. It's at Ms. Johnson's place, drying out."

Cade lowered his head to peer into the vehicle. "Ms. Johnson?"

"From Pete Bolton's ranch," she clarified.

"This is my half brother, Cade Redstone. Cade, this is Heather Johnson."

Cade stretched a tanned arm in front of Mitch, and Heather shook his hand. "What's this about drying out your truck?"

"I'll explain it to you later," Mitch said.

"Uh-oh. Has the dynamic duo been at it again?"

"Big-time." Mitch got out and opened the back door to help unbuckle his daughters. They ran off toward the house.

"Thanks again," Mitch said, ducking in the passenger window. "I'll be out tomorrow to fix that fence. Sorry for the inconvenience."

His directly appreciative gaze caught Heather up short. She wasn't in the market for anything other than a remodeling job, and he didn't even fit those qualifications. She shrugged. "No rush. The horses were boarded at a neighbor's before I arrived."

"You know where I am if you change your mind about the project."

She nodded noncommittally. Besides how disturbed she felt in his presence, his children were more trouble than she needed. "Goodbye."

He moved away and she steered the Blazer back toward the highway. She'd been thinking about considering his offer when they'd heard the commotion from outside. Thank goodness she hadn't made a quick decision based on her instantaneous reaction to his appearance. She didn't trust a man who couldn't handle two small children to manage a remodeling project.

Somebody else was sure to call about the job.

Three

No one else called about the job. Heather had tried every number in Whitehorn's leaflet that someone had amusingly labeled a phone directory, without finding anyone willing to take on the repair work. One local company offered to place her on their waiting list, but wouldn't promise anything until November.

She couldn't wait that long. She couldn't wait any longer. Once she even found a contractor, the work would take weeks. Her vacation was over and she had been forced to ask for a leave of absence until matters were settled. Her boss had pressed her for a return date, but she'd been unable to provide him with one. She had to get things moving quickly or she worried her job would be in jeopardy.

The children had been in bed for more than an hour, the laundry was done, and Heather made herself a cup of tea and carried it out to the porch. She went back in for a sweatshirt before snuggling down in the comfortable rattan rocker that creaked beneath her weight.

The clatter of the frogs sounded more like locusts than the deep-throated croak one expected. At the sound, long-buried memories edged to the surface of her mind and she recalled the summer evenings of her childhood. She'd been alone. Always alone. After her mother's death, her father had retreated into a bottle and turned her care over to his dominating housekeeper.

Heather had despised the woman and at every opportunity had hidden herself away to avoid her. Coming back to the ranch after so many years raised memories better left forgotten. With strict discipline, she locked away those unpleasant thoughts.

Her husband had never been much of a father. He'd paid minimal attention to Patrick at first, since he'd been the first boy, but the novelty had soon worn off. Craig had made money. That had been his forte. But he'd believed Heather should be making money, too. They couldn't afford the life-style and the house and the status he thought they needed on one salary.

And Heather had never minded working, since her job gave her the satisfaction and self-worth she'd never received at home. Sometimes she'd had misgivings about the time away from her family, about the firsts she had missed, and the opportunities that slipped by, but it was just the way things were for everyone these days.

Her boss had called tonight, conferring with her on a project due in another month. His reliance on her expertise assured her of her value in the company. They were impatient for her to settle this situation. Everyone had family matters arise from time to time;

however, companies were understanding only to a point.

Unfortunately, Mitch Fielding's offer was the only option she had at this time. That or selling the ranch off in its present condition and losing a heck of a profit. Heaven knew she could use the money from the sale of the ranch to make life easier. Craig paid child support, but her apartment cost a small fortune and there were always unforeseen expenses with a family.

Their house hadn't been paid for, so she'd let him take over the payments. He'd married again within a year.

Not her. She got by just fine without someone to stifle and criticize her every move, thank you very much. She almost felt sorry for Craig's new wife, who obviously hadn't known the oppression she was bowing under when she'd spoken those vows.

No, this was the life for her. She tucked her feet under her and sipped her tea. And as soon as she got back to San Francisco, everything would be back to normal—better than normal actually.

How long could the remodeling take, anyway? Could Mitch hurry along contractors? She would have to make it clear that expediency was part of the deal. No waiting around for weeks and weeks to get things done. She planned the tactics in her head—how she would make the arrangement, how long she would give him, and how soon the work would be under way.

And as for his children—what were two more little girls?

Mitch had been replacing wires and checking belts under the hood of his truck for about an hour when the pewter-colored Blazer pulled up into the graveled area. Heather got out, sent Jessica and Patrick into the house, and came over to talk to him, carrying her youngest. Mitch couldn't help noticing the young mother's shapely legs revealed by a pair of cuffed white shorts. His gaze skimmed up the length of those slender legs to her slim waist.

"Get it running?" she asked. Her shoulder-length honey-brown hair glistened with streaks of blond in the sunlight. She wore a sleeveless sweater with a row of tiny buttons that drew his attention to nicely rounded breasts beneath the fabric. The soft shade of blue made her golden eyes sparkle once she pushed her sunglasses up onto her head. The baby's hand rested on the swell of one breast and Mitch's throat got so dry, he had to look away.

He wiped his hands on a rag. "Pretty rough, but it's running. I figured I'd have it towed to get it out of your yard, if it didn't start."

"It's not bothering anything," she replied. She glanced around the yard. "You fixed the corral."

"First thing."

Her unreadable gaze fluttered to the barn and back. "Mitch."

His name from her lips pleased him in some unexplainable way. He liked the sound. "Yeah."

"Your suggestions were better than any of the other candidates's. I've decided to negotiate with you on the remodeling project. There are a few things we need to get straight first, and I have a list of questions."

"My time is your time," he said amenably.

"Have you had lunch?"

"Not yet."

"Please join us. After we eat, we'll sit on the porch, such as it is, and talk business."

He gave a nod. "All right."

"Where are your daughters?"

"Cade agreed to look after them. He's a newlywed and his wife Leanne teased that he could use the practice."

"He seems like a nice guy."

"Very. I'm glad we got together. With my other half brothers, too. It's been an interesting experience. Whether or not I get any land isn't really important. Discovering I have family is."

She tucked a length of hair behind her ear and looked away, as if the personal subject made her uncomfortable. She adjusted Andrew on her hip and the boy's hand dropped from her breast. Mitch made himself look at her eyes. Equally as disturbing.

"About twenty-five minutes, then?" she asked.

He refocused on their conversation. "I'll be there."

Almost an hour later she carried two frosted glasses

of iced tea out to the porch and they settled on the
weathered furniture. She crossed her smooth, distract-
ing legs. She had to know what a distraction that was,
but she seemed to not notice his perusal. Her toes
peeked from her sandals, revealing delicate nails
painted a pale pink.

Mitch purposely studied one of the barn cats that
lay in a sliver of sunlight. The feline gave him a dis-
interested blink and flicked his tail against the porch
floor in a rhythmic beat.

"First, it's important that you know I'm under time
pressure to get this done and get back home,"
Heather told Mitch.

"I understand." He'd never met anyone who
wasn't in a hurry to get a construction project finished. "There's quite a bit I can do on my own," he
said. "But the more help I can hire, the faster it'll go.
But since money is tight, we can't bring in too many
workers."

"How many will speed things up?"

"Even two or three would help a lot."

"Can I afford them?"

"I'll contract them. That way they'll be getting
paid as the work progresses, even though I won't get
paid until the sale goes through. How's that?"

She looked surprised. "That's more than I expected. You wouldn't survive a week in San Francisco, doing business this way."

"You can get ripped off by paying for services
ahead of the finished work," he replied, thinking she

was biting the hand that fed her if that had been crit-
icism.

"Noted," she said with a nod.

"Let's decide how extensive you want this reno-
vation, and make a budget."

Again she looked surprised, as though she hadn't
expected him to be this professional. After seeing his
ineptitude with his kids, her surprise might be justi-
fied, he thought wryly.

She walked him through the house, and he took
notes and made lists on the tablet in his black folder.
He asked her questions and made suggestions until
their ideas for the project were compatible.

They entered the wood-floored living room where
the kids were sprawled on sleeping bags, watching a
cartoon.

"Do you have a computer?" he asked.

She nodded. "I brought it with me so I could
work."

"Good. I have a program for designing kitchens
and baths that you can play with. You give it the
specs, lay out the requirements, and it designs the
blueprints. Saves a lot of money and the plans are
easy to work from. I've used it dozens of times. Let's
go outside."

She nodded and they walked out to survey the
house and outbuildings together.

"The house is good and solid, and the land is valu-
able. Your father had a nice operation going here at

one time. I would think it would be hard to sell and leave it all to strangers.''

She glanced at the cloudless blue sky, then down the length of the drive. ''I have a good job waiting for me.''

Not an explanation. Not a word about any sentimental ties or feelings of regret at selling. Nothing personal at all. He'd been neatly kept at a distance. Her impersonal treatment shouldn't have bothered him; he was a professional. But it did. For some reason what she thought of him mattered. And she obviously didn't think him worthy of her thoughts or feelings.

He took her cue and stayed on the subject of the work. Another hour later he climbed into his truck, praying it would start again, and gave her a salute when the engine turned over and he drove off.

Beneath the plastic sheeting the seat was wet, and the once-blue carpeting was green and slimy. The whole cab smelled like skunky water. He'd called around and found a place willing to clean the interior, but it wasn't going to be cheap. There was still the matter of the creased fender, too.

Taylor and Ashley would never make enough allowance in their combined lifetimes to pay for this fiasco, and he still wasn't sure how to handle their behavior. Last night, he'd given them each a stern lecture and grounded them to their room. He and the girls shared a room in Garrett's house, which Mitch had twin-proofed, so there had been no way to separate them. Since they'd had each other, he wasn't sure just how effective the evening's confinement had been.

Besides, he thought, pulling into the drive, taking them to Cade and Leanne's today had given them another reprieve.

He found the three of them on the side lawn, engaged in a chaotic game of croquet. Cade merely shook his head, rubbed his shin, and turned the girls over to their father.

"Thanks, man," Mitch said. "I owe you one."

"You owe me two," his half brother replied with a wry grin.

Mitch agreed with a laugh, belted the girls into the borrowed ranch truck, and drove to his grandfather's ranch.

"Daddy, we're bored," Ashley said, jumping out of the truck and bouncing on the balls of her feet.

"I have to take my truck to get it cleaned, and you two are grounded."

"But you left us all day!" Taylor said, wide-eyed.

"Don't tell me you didn't have a good time with Uncle Cade."

"But we want to go get some ice cream. It's boring here."

As usual, Mitch couldn't bring himself to be harder, because he felt sorry for them. They had no mother. Somehow these incidents just never seemed important enough to disrupt life more, to make his girls even more unhappy.

Ashley pouted and plopped herself on the lawn, her grass-stained knees drawn up to her chin. Taylor took his hand and pumped it persistently. What had happened to those darling, angelic babies? When had they become manipulators?

"All right. Let's go get some ice cream."

"And rent a movie, Daddy?" Ashley begged.

He wasn't doing the right thing, but he didn't know what to do, and he didn't know how to change this cycle of behavior. The twins were confused. This was another new situation, and they'd been faced with so many adjustments in their short lives.

He hoped that once the work started at the Bolton ranch, his girls wouldn't make the days miserable for all of them. He just had no idea how to ensure that.

Arranging bids and hiring his helpers took most of the week, but by the following Monday, work was under way. Mitch had pulled a lot of strings and taken advantage of small-town kindness to hasten the progress, and Heather appreciated his efforts.

He and the three men he'd hired had been tearing off the back porch and the shingles most of the morning. Heather figured she'd better get used to the racket; this was only the first day.

She'd shopped in Billings and ordered via the Internet to acquire materials to teach and entertain five children for several weeks. Organization was the key to keeping things running smoothly, so she'd scheduled their days on a calendar with classes and crafts and playtime.

This morning, Taylor slumped in her chair and refused to participate. She glared at Heather. "You can't make me."

"You're right, I guess. I can't make you. You'll just have to sit there and be bored."

Taylor folded her arms over her chest and belligerently raised her chin. "I want to watch a video."

"It's not video time until after lunch."

Taylor scowled and kicked the table leg with her swinging foot.

Heather took a deep breath and turned back to the table. A few minutes later, while showing Patrick how to connect the numbered dots on a page, she heard Taylor jump up from the table.

The child ran for the back door—the door they'd all been warned not to use—twisted the bolt and threw open the door. A scream ripped from her throat as she disappeared from sight.

Heather reached the opening and stared four feet down at the pile of boards and rubble where the girl had landed. "Taylor! Are you all right?"

Mitch scrambled down the ladder from where he'd been ripping off boards and bounded over the debris to his daughter. Crying indignantly, the child sat and raised her bleeding knee.

"Honey, didn't you hear me tell all of you not to come out that door?" he asked.

Heather stared down at the top of his head. "She heard you, all right."

He glanced up. "What happened?"

Taylor wiped hair away from her eyes and glared at Heather. "She's mean. I don't like her. I wanna go back to our grampa's ranch."

"Taylor, Heather is not mean. You can't go back until we all go back together tonight. Heather is taking care of you during the day while I work. I explained that."

She managed to make her chin quiver. "She tried to make me draw pictures I don't want to color."

Mitch propped a small ladder from the ground to the doorway above. He picked up Taylor. "Let's get this cut cleaned and bandaged."

Heather moved back and watched him enter the kitchen and sit his daughter on the chair she'd earlier occupied.

"Look what I made, Daddy." Ashley held up the picture she'd drawn.

Mitch praised her artwork and accepted the plastic first-aid kit Heather supplied. He paused in cleaning his daughter's knee to survey Heather's expression.

Feeling helpless, she merely raised a brow. He must feel this way all the time.

Taylor immediately started to cry again. "My leg hurts!"

Mitch met Heather's gaze, his confusion obvious. "Here, let me get a bandage on, and you can go rest for a while."

"Can I watch a video?"

"Sure, as long as you're sitting quietly."

Over his shoulder, Taylor gave Heather a smug look and allowed her tears to subside.

Heather did a slow burn. "It's still lesson time," she said. "I planned videos for after lunch."

Mitch straightened. "Couldn't we bend the schedule just a little to accommodate today's problems?"

"May I have a word with you alone?" she asked.

"Can I have a cookie, too?" Taylor asked.

Mitch glanced from his daughter to Heather.

"They haven't had lunch yet," she supplied.

"Excuse us for a minute," Mitch said. "Girls, you sit here while I talk to Heather."

Wondering all the while what she'd gotten herself into, Heather followed him into the living room. He led the way, as though he'd taken charge of this situation, and his assumption ruffled her.

"It seems to me that constantly bending the schedule—and the rules—is the main problem here," she said in a low, controlled voice.

His expression darkened. "Don't get me wrong," he said. "I know they're not angels. I haven't known what to do with them most of the time. But I think they need a little flexibility."

"Maybe it's stability they need."

His eyes seemed to soften. And his voice, when he spoke again, was laced with a combination of vulnerability and tenderness. "Can't there be both?"

Four

Heather took a deep breath. She was a stickler for details, she knew that. She functioned best with order and discipline. Her children had always done fine under her leadership. But they had seemed to blossom more since they'd been at the ranch—since their days weren't consumed with rigorous schedules. Perhaps there was a compromise.

She drew herself up and looked Mitch in the eye. "All right."

She led the way back to the kitchen. "We'll take a break and have some free time," she said to the children. "You can watch a video or draw or anything you want until lunch."

The kids looked at each other and grinned cheerfully.

Mitch gave her a grateful smile, then turned to have a few words with his girls. Within minutes he headed back outside.

By lunch Heather's nerves were still on edge. She prepared sandwiches and sliced fruit and ushered the children out the front door for a picnic on the side lawn, where they could be entertained watching the workers.

"I don't like tuna," Taylor complained, peeling back her bread and wrinkling her nose.

"Me neither," Ashley agreed. "I want skettios."

"I'll get some skettios for later in the week, but for now, we're having tuna."

"I don't like it," they chorused.

"Then don't eat it."

They looked at one another and blinked. Taylor looked back. "You're not gonna make us eat it?"

"Nope."

Taylor nestled onto the checkered tablecloth as though she'd won a battle. "What do we get, then?"

"There are chips on your plate and apple and orange slices."

"That's not a good lunch."

"Everyone else is eating it." Heather demonstrated by taking a bite of her sandwich. Patrick and Andrew were watching the exchange with interest while they chewed. Jessica already looked as tired of the girls' complaints as Heather felt.

Ashley stared, agape. "But we'll be hungry!"

"I guess you will."

Taylor folded her arms over her chest and pouted.

The afternoon went a little more smoothly, because she'd purchased Veggie-Tales' videos none of them had seen before. The kids watched and laughed, and at snack time, nobody complained about raisins, graham crackers, or juice.

"Now it's time to pick everything up and put it away," Heather announced.

"I'm not pickin' stuff up. My leg hurts." Taylor ensconced herself on the sofa.

Her leg had been fine all afternoon, Heather noted. "Everyone who helps, gets a treat," she coaxed, thinking that would bring the girl around.

The others picked up puzzles and toys and rolled up the sleeping bags they liked to lounge upon, then Heather presented four of the five children with a heart-shaped treat from her private stash of Godiva chocolates.

Taylor scowled, pursed her lips into a pout, and glared at Heather. "You're mean. I don't like you."

"I'm sorry you feel that way. You had the same chance as the others to help clean up."

"I'm just a kid."

"You're not just a kid. You're a very bright and capable young lady." With a negative attitude.

"What's 'capable'?"

"It means you're smart and good at doing things."

Apparently the compliment from someone she considered mean confused her. She leaned back on the aged sofa, refusing to watch the others finish their candy. Probably planning a dramatic tale with which to regale her father, Heather thought. "My daddy will buy me a treat of my own."

While Patrick and Andrew took naps upstairs, Heather gave the three girls a stack of books, put on a tape of relaxing rainforest sounds, and with one ear zeroed on the chatter, familiarized herself with the blueprint program Mitch had given her on disk.

It was as easy as he'd assured her, and she enjoyed experimenting with the different kitchen scenarios. Before long, she'd narrowed it down to two floor plans. She would show them to him for his input on cost-effectiveness.

Heather rearranged the room again, making space for the washer and dryer to be enclosed. She checked the clock, saved her work to a disk, and went to check on the kids.

Taylor sat on a worn chair and slid down until her chin reached her chest. "I don't wanna be here."

Her heart softened toward the troublesome child. She picked up a book from the floor and perched on the sofa. "I guess this is different from the way things used to be for you, isn't it?"

Blue eyes assessed her skeptically.

"I'll bet you miss your grandmas, huh?"

Taylor allowed a fractional nod.

"And our mama," Ashley said from the other side of the room. "We miss our mama, don't we, Taylor?"

One side of Taylor's mouth moved up in what might have been agreement.

"Did your mother read to you?" Heather asked, hoping to find a way to connect with the little girl.

"Yes, she did. She read to us all the time. Every night. Good books, too, not dumb ones."

"Would you like it if I read a story to you?"

Taylor's expression remained unchanged.

"I would!" Immediately Ashley came and seated

herself right beside Heather, delightedly worming her way until she was nearly in her lap.

Heather met Jessica's look of amusement and they shared a grin. Obviously Jess recognized what Heather had been trying to do and sympathized.

Heather pulled the eager, loving child into her lap and opened the book. So easy. It was so easy for this twin to ingratiate herself, to show her need for closeness and a maternal touch.

Taylor watched from her position on the chair. She didn't seem to resent her sister's gregarious ability to tuck herself into an embrace and enjoy herself, but surely her thoughts were confused. Heather got confused just watching her.

Jess came to sit beside them and listen to the story, too. Taylor listened without expression.

When the boys awoke, Heather took the children outdoors for the rest of the afternoon. They sat for a while on the grassy bank of the pond, watching dragonflies and tossing sticks into the water. The pounding of hammers drew her gaze to the house where Mitch and his three-man crew, having removed the old roof and torn off the back porch, were framing the new one.

The house was located in an ideal spot, with a view of the Crazy Mountains off to the northwest. Years ago there had been a garden on that same side of the house; Heather remembered picking beans in the morning sun.

A cyclone fence would be ideal for a family home,

she mused. Children could be left to play safely inside
with a swing set and a sandbox. Mentally ticking off
the remaining weeks, she wondered if a few playground toys wouldn't be a good investment toward
keeping her sanity.

The hired men worked until nearly eight, then
headed toward Whitehorn. "You're welcome to the
shower," she told Mitch. "And I have some supper
saved if you'd like it."

"I brought a change of clothes, so I'll take you up
on that." Minutes later he returned with damp hair,
his skin darkened from a day in the sun.

"I wanted to show you the plans I came up with
today." She pointed to the pages she'd printed and
placed on the table. She filled a plate from the dishes
in the oven.

Mitch studied her floor plans. "I like this one a lot.
But you know, if we sort of combined the two and
added on just a couple of feet out that way—" he
gestured with a thumb "—we could include a shower
in the laundry room. And a door from outside. That
way Mr. Rancher could come in after his long dirty
day and not even have to walk through the house."

"That's a practical suggestion," she said after a
moment's thought. "I like it a lot, and it would really
add to the appeal of the place. How much?"

He jotted a few columns on the back of the paper,
tallied them and gave her a figure. "Ball park," he
said. "Nothing fancy—molded shower stall."

She nodded. "Let's do it."

Mitch dug into the food she'd placed before him. It was an unaccustomed pleasure to have a lovely and attentive young woman serve him his supper. He'd missed this normal kind of life.

Heather moved around the kitchen, her motions graceful and efficient. He pictured her in a power suit, sitting in an office in a high-rise building. What a change this must be for her. "How did your day go?" he asked. "The rest of your day, anyway?"

She hung a dish towel to dry. "Fair, considering I have no idea how to get through to Taylor."

She told him about the problems she had with her, and about Taylor's reactions. "Don't be surprised if she asks you to buy her a treat."

He swallowed and pushed the plate aside. She was knocking herself out here, and as always, his kids weren't cooperating. "Thanks for being understanding about the video today."

Sitting across from him, she folded her hands on the tabletop and leaned forward slightly. "I'm trying to be understanding. But the girls need a sense of guidance and direction from you. I need to know that you're going to back me up on my techniques."

She was getting too close to identifying his dilemma and his feelings of inadequacy. He folded his napkin and got up to pour himself a cup of coffee. He sat back down, avoiding her eyes.

"Sugar?" she asked.

"What? Oh, yes, thank you." He stirred a spoonful into his cup. There was nothing she could tell him about his kids's acting out that he didn't know. "I know their behavior is...embarrassing."

"Is that what you call it?"

He set his lips in a firm line, feeling defensive. "I've done the best I've known how since their mother died. Children shouldn't have to be without a mother. They were so small..."

Her lovely eyes were filled with compassion, not condemnation. "I'm sorry they lost their mother."

Mitch shrugged, not knowing what to say, how to explain. His uncertainty and mismanagement was another embarrassment, and he didn't particularly want to reveal his insecurities to this woman who seemed to have her life and her children so neatly pulled together. Life's situations weren't always black-and-white, cut-and-dried, and he'd already told her more about himself than he was certain she cared to know.

He understood her reasoning, he really did. He just didn't want to lay down boundaries that he would once again end up moving. It was less stressful to give in immediately than to try to take a stand and have his determination broken down with cries and tears that made him feel guilty and rotten. And that was how it always ended.

"Children need limits, Mitch," she said softly. "Neither parent nor child benefits from letting the child determine the rules."

Her calm reasoning had begun to irritate him. She had no idea what their life had been like. It was not her place to sit in judgment over his parenting. "I can handle my kids," he said a little too defensively.

She placed both hands flat on the table. "Not when you're working, you can't. If I'm going to be their caregiver, then you've got to trust me with some of their discipline."

"As long as it's reasonable," he replied.

"Are you suggesting I'm being unreasonable?"

"I didn't say that."

Heather ran a slim hand through her hair in obvious frustration.

If she'd had the option of changing her mind about keeping the girls, she probably would have, he thought. He knew how exhausting they were, what a challenge. His own sense of failure was so great, his words were hollow even to his own ears.

"Just remember," she said finally, "that your choices can make it harder for me—for all of us—day by day. And your girls have a whole lifetime ahead of them to try to get along with other people who won't be catering to their every whim."

"They're only six," was all he could think to say. There were years and years ahead for them to have to deal with the world.

She stood and waved a hand toward the other room where the kids played, as if dismissing him.

Mitch headed in that direction and returned with his troublesome daughter. "Taylor, tell Heather you're sorry for being difficult today."

"This isn't necessary," Heather said.

He studied Taylor patiently.

"Do I have to?"

"Yes."

Taylor took him seriously for a change. Another scene was the last thing he needed or wanted, and Heather was trying.

"Sorry," she said, stubbing the toe of her tennis shoe on the floor with a series of squeaks.

"Thank you for apologizing," Heather replied. "Let's just forget today and start over. Okay?"

Taylor took her father's hand and stared adoringly up into his face. "Will you buy me a treat on the way home?"

He wanted to run before Heather could see any more of Taylor's manipulations. Mitch reached out his other hand for Ashley. "It's late, let's get going. Thank you, Heather. We'll see you in the morning."

"All right," she replied, and saw them out the screen door. "Good night."

"Are we, Daddy?" Taylor inquired. "Are we getting a treat now?"

He led them to the borrowed ranch truck, telling himself Heather was right. He'd known it all along, but hadn't been able to put discipline into action, because he'd been thinking wrong. Letting them get away with murder wasn't doing them any favors.

He saw to it that they fastened their seat belts, and climbed in behind the steering wheel.

"Daddy, I want some ice cream."

"Taylor, you didn't mind Heather today, like I

asked you to.'' He took a deep breath and started the truck. "I don't think you deserve a treat."

He could almost hear her blinking in consternation in the dark interior. "But I wanna treat. The others got chocolate."

"Did you help pick up the toys like they did?"

"Nuh-uh, Daddy," Ashley supplied. "She din't want to."

"Is that right, Taylor?"

She didn't reply. She started to cry. Sitting on the side by the door, she slumped down in the seat as far as she could go in the seat belt. "Heather's me-heean. She's a ta-hattle tale."

"No she's not. She's responsible for you while I'm working."

"She's not my boss."

"She has my permission to be your boss while you're there with her."

"I can't sleep tonight without ice cream. My tummy's hungry."

Feeling more sorry for Ashley than for himself, Mitch flicked the knobs on the dash, finding the radio dead. It was going to be a long ride. And a long evening until his children fell asleep.

Five

Heather wondered while she bathed the kids and dressed them for bed, what had taken place in Mitch's truck on the way home. It was a long drive to have to listen to squalling if he'd refused Taylor's request.

Jessica read a book to the boys and Heather listened, then tucked them all in. Patrick and Andrew were sharing a room and a bed. Andrew still slept in a crib at home, so she'd purchased a mesh guard for the side of the mattress to keep him from falling off.

The toys they'd brought were neatly stored in laundry baskets and cardboard boxes, and their clothes lined the drawers of the antique chest.

Jessica seemed to consider their stay a pleasant diversion, though she'd mentioned missing her school friends who'd occasionally spent the night. She had rearranged a small room into her own space, and had spread her teddy bear collection across a window seat.

The children had adjusted to the visit amazingly well, actually enjoying the slow pace and the outdoors.

"Couldn't we bring some of Grandpa's horses back to the ranch?" Jess asked as Heather spread the sheet over her and tucked it under the mattress.

"I don't have time to take care of horses," Heather told her for the third time. "They take a lot of work and eat a lot."

"We could try, couldn't we?"

"I suppose we could if we wanted to be ranchers. But our home is in San Francisco. We'll be going back in a few weeks."

Her daughter tucked her favorite teddy bear beneath her chin and rubbed his synthetic fur. "I saw other kids riding horses when we were coming back from Billings. It sure looks fun."

A pang of guilt rose up in Heather and made her think twice. After all, bending her plans to give her daughter harmless pleasure was no big sacrifice. She could take a stab at being flexible. "I suppose I can arrange for you to go riding while we're here. Would you like that?"

Jess nodded and grinned.

"Want the door open a crack?"

"No. I kinda like the light from the moon shining in the window."

Heather kissed her forehead. "Good night, sweetie."

"'Night, Mom."

Heather went to her room, changed into a sleep shirt, and picked up a book. After a few minutes of trying to concentrate, she got up and wandered down the silent hall.

The room the boys slept in had been hers as a child. She observed their peaceful slumber in the sliver of moonlight that striped the line-dried sheets they curled beneath.

The room held no memories for them; the house, no ghosts, and they slept in innocent repose. Upon her arrival, Heather had scrubbed every inch of every room and washed every faded curtain, rug and quilt, as if she could wipe out the lonely echoes that hid in the corners, erase the bleak memories that waited in the shadows.

Assured that the ghosts were hers alone, she descended the stairs and made her way out the front door. Beneath her bare feet, the ground still held the warmth of the sun. Light-sensitive floodlights artificially chased away the darkness in bright pools in front of the barn and stables.

Frogs chirped from their hiding places near the pond. A night owl mourned a pitiful cry. Fireflies dotted the hayfields and a barn cat slunk across the pool of light circling the front of the stable.

There had been horses. Hundreds of them in the pasturelands, the corrals, the stalls of the barn. On nights like this, as a child, she'd stolen away to escape the house and her father's housekeeper. She had vague memories of an old cowboy who sometimes saddled a horse for her. But more often, until she'd grown big enough to lift the saddles herself, she'd ridden bareback.

Night after night, she'd slipped from the house unnoticed and escaped into the countryside. The animals always knew their way back, sometimes to her disappointment, when she wanted only to ride until Montana was a speck on the horizon behind her.

She'd made her break finally, Heather thought wryly, sitting on a boulder near the edge of the pond and pulling her knees up under her nightshirt. She'd made certain of it her last year of high school. Craig had been a driven young man, with high ideals and goals, having completed two years at the community college and ready to leave for the university on the west coast.

When Heather became pregnant, Craig had dutifully married her and taken her with him. Heather had believed she was escaping, but she'd only traded one prison for another.

Coming back to Montana threatened her newfound independence. She didn't want to be here—and she didn't want to remember why anymore. A nighttime ride had an appeal all its own, she thought, wistfully remembering the heady sense of freedom.

Studying the newly framed and roofed back porch, she liked the addition. Mitch had made the porch deeper to accommodate outdoor furniture, and built twelve-foot-wide stairs that would hold potted plants. Maybe she'd pick up a few so the perspective buyers could see the appeal.

The faint rumble of thunder rolled in the distance and she headed for the house. A light shower would be welcome, but she prayed rain wouldn't impede the progress on the remodeling.

Her life in San Francisco awaited. There was nothing for her here—never had been. Why, then, did the image of a sandy-haired, blue-eyed, overstressed dad come to mind?

Taylor wore an expression as dark and foreboding as the thunderclouds that hung low in the morning sky. She gave Heather a look that was intended to blister eyeballs, and sullenly seated herself at the kitchen table with Jessica and Patrick. Ashley took a seat on the floor beside Andrew and watched him drop metal cars through his miniature basketball hoop.

"No outside work today," Heather said to Mitch, wanting instead to ask if she'd guessed correctly and that Taylor's black attitude was because she hadn't gotten her treat on the way home the night before.

"No, and I can't tear out that upstairs bath until I've added the new one down here. I can't add the new one down here until we get a nice day to tear out that exterior wall. My bad weather options are repairing walls, replacing woodwork or painting."

Heather glanced at the rain drizzling down the windowpane. "Might as well start in the living room or the office."

"How about both? We can take care of those today. Where do you want stuff moved to?"

She led him into the living room. "This area is big enough to just push everything into the middle while you work, don't you think?"

The look he gave her was disturbing, because she

had to wonder if he was even thinking of the day's work. His eyes scanned her hair and face, and one side of his appealing mouth inched up in a crooked grin.

A spicy masculine scent that was uniquely his drifted on the air to tease her. He wore a clean pair of jeans and a striped T-shirt today, ordinary clothing that looked anything but ordinary on him. Noticing these things was so unlike her, she had shocked herself. She turned quickly, and he followed her into the dining room. She could almost feel his gaze on her back.

"There's room in here if you want to temporarily move the file cabinets and desk from the office." She flicked a wall switch. "I never have figured out what this goes to."

He stepped closer and her heart groped in search of a steady beat. She reached to balance herself with a hand on the yellow-papered wall, then felt foolish.

"I'll take a look at it when we get to this room," he said. He was paying attention to the job, and she'd lost her mind.

"Well." She placed her hands on her hips. "The kids and I will stay in the kitchen and upstairs today," she said. "Maybe I'll take them into Whitehorn for lunch. They'll no doubt get restless."

"Are you sure you want to risk taking them all to the café?" he asked, a skeptical frown creasing his brow. "The girls are a handful."

"You let me do my job and I'll let you do yours,"

she said with a staunch grin, not at all confident about her ability to keep the twins in line. But an entire day closed up with the smell of paint and putty and the combustible energy of five active children was even less appealing. Then there was the distraction of having this man to look at. She would brave the café.

Mitch had his helpers repair walls and woodwork, while he measured the rooms for carpet and laid tile in front of the door. They had the two rooms patched and sanded by late afternoon when Heather returned.

The sky had cleared and a rainbow stretched across the huddled mountain peaks in the distance. Mitch met her as she parked her Blazer and opened the doors for the kids to spill out.

"How'd it go?" he asked.

"I'm going to need a vacation when this vacation is over," she said without much amusement.

"Did you have lunch at the café?"

She nodded. "We only had one small calamity when Ashley tipped back the chair she was sitting in. We couldn't all fit into a booth."

"Is she okay?"

"She's fine. She was embarrassed mostly."

"I'll reimburse you." He took out his wallet. "You left a big tip."

"How'd you know?"

He raised a brow. "I've taken them places. I know you'd rather crawl under a rock than have the poor waitress see the mess before you can get out the door."

She accepted the bill he extended. "Done for the day?"

"Yup." He'd already cleaned up and sent the others home. Garrett had specifically asked him to be at the ranch for supper that evening. "I'll be taking the girls and heading out," he said. "I'll get an early start tomorrow." Tomorrow the patched spots would be dry enough to paint. "You'll need to go pick out carpeting."

"So soon?"

"Figured we might as well do it before we moved the furniture back."

"Might as well. See you tomorrow." She held Andrew's hand and walked him up the new back steps. Mitch watched their progress for a few minutes, his attention mostly on the way Heather filled out a pair of shorts.

The twins chattered and asked questions all the way to the ranch. At least his own truck had a stereo, so he could play music, which sometimes soothed their restlessness on the long ride.

Suzanne Harding, the ranch foreman's wife, waved to Mitch from the front porch. He parked and helped the girls out.

"Hi, Mitch," Suzanne called. Her dark auburn-highlighted hair was caught up in an attractive twist.

Mitch greeted her.

"Where's Joe?" Ashley asked enthusiastically. She'd taken an immediate liking to Rand and Suzanne's baby boy.

"He's in the kitchen with Hattie," she replied, referring to Garrett's newest cook and housekeeper.

The girls squealed and threw open the front door, jostling each other to be the first inside.

"I'm hoping Taylor and Ashley can come to our place for supper and to play this evening," Suzanne said. "My girlfriend is bringing her daughter and I thought the three of them would hit it off."

"I don't know," Mitch said skeptically.

"I know, I know," she said. "I've heard all the circulating stories about the girls, but we get along fine."

Hearing that his children were the subjects of conversation all over the county, Mitch cringed inwardly.

"They rode to the house with me once and we didn't have a problem, remember?" she went on.

An evening all to himself appealed more than she could know. Others only *heard* the stories—he lived them.

Mitch glanced at his watch. He'd worked a shorter day than usual, so a few quiet hours stretched temptingly in front of him. "If you're sure," he said hesitantly.

"I'm sure."

"Well, all right."

"Good. I'll let them know and pack them up. My car's out back. Oh, your grandfather wants to see you. He's in the foal barn."

Mitch nodded and thanked her, then made his way

across the distance to the barns and found his grandfather mixing feed for one of the mares.

Garrett straightened and grinned at Mitch. "How's the work going on the Bolton place?"

"Had to work inside today. Made some progress though."

Garrett removed his gloves and tucked them into his back pocket. "I've set up a meeting with Jordan Baxter. I'm hoping we can settle this thing out of court."

"It'll be all right if this doesn't turn out." Mitch tried to assure him, wishing for his sake that Garrett wasn't so emotionally involved in the land battle.

"That land is your legacy," his grandfather said. "It's been in the family for generations, and you and your brothers each deserve a slice of it. I'm not going to rest until Kincaid land is back in the hands of its rightful owners."

That was what Mitch had figured. Though the hair that was dark in the photographs on the mantel was now silver, his grandfather seemed relatively healthy. His skin was tanned from hours in the saddle and his blue eyes twinkled with good humor and generosity.

Mitch could see nothing of himself in the features Garrett Kincaid had inherited from his Native American grandmother. Not like his thirty-year-old half bother, Collin, who was a younger version of Garrett.

"I've invited company for dinner, so we need to change," Garrett said, switching the subject.

Mitch glanced at his jeans and cotton shirt.

"You need to start meeting people," the old man said with a decisive nod. "Six-thirty sharp."

Mitch shrugged and accompanied him to the house, where they went their separate ways.

At six-thirty, he joined Garrett in his study. The man had dressed in black slacks and a deep red shirt with a silver-and-turquoise bolo tie at his throat. Mitch's navy trousers and cream-colored shirt were less dramatic, but equally handsome. Collin joined them, his dark hair and blue eyes set off by a white shirt and gray jacket.

"Hey, Mitch," he said, good-naturedly slapping his back. "Where are those blonde bombshells?"

"Suzanne asked if they could go home with her for the evening. I couldn't resist the offer."

Collin chuckled. As Larry's legitimate son, he'd been more than welcoming to Mitch and the rest of the newly discovered Kincaid heirs. Obviously, Garrett had set a fair and just example, because Collin was as determined as his grandfather to see his half brothers get their share of the land.

"So, who's coming to dinner?" Mitch asked.

The doorbell rang just then, and Garrett hurried to answer it. He returned with a tall young woman who wore her dark hair pulled back in a severe bun. Glasses didn't hide the curiosity in her dark brown eyes.

"Summer, this is your distant cousin, Mitch. Mitch, Summer Kincaid is my first cousin Jeremiah's grand-daughter."

Garrett had explained the family tree several times, but Mitch still got confused over who was related to whom. Summer bore the unmistakable characteristics of her Cheyenne father.

Another young woman accompanied her, a slender, ivory-skinned blonde wearing a short red dress and silver sandals.

"And this is Trina McCann," Summer said. "She's a friend of mine."

Mitch greeted both young women politely, and after a few minutes, Hattie called them in to dinner.

The table had been set more formally than usual, and from his position at the head of the table, Garrett graciously poured wine and carved beef. Collin had seated himself beside Summer, which left Mitch and Trina on the other side of the table.

She asked him questions about his home in Minnesota and he answered, all the while wondering at this odd dinner gathering. Garrett had obviously planned it in advance, even though Mitch normally had the girls with him. He began to suspect it hadn't been a coincidence that Suzanne had shown up and spirited the twins away this particular evening. Mitch met Garrett's blue eyes and read only kindness in their depths.

Mitch studied his dinner partner more carefully. One side of her fair shoulder-length hair was pinned up with a glittery barrette. She was petite, but curvy, with wide blue eyes and a gregarious personality. She gave Mitch a coquettish smile from beneath dark lashes.

He had revealed to his grandfather that one day he'd like to meet someone and marry again. But he'd never dreamed that the old man would take it upon himself to assist that process.

"No reason for you young people to end your evening early," Garrett said after they'd had coffee in the comfortable living room.

"What do you say we tip a few at the Branding Iron?" Collin asked genially.

Mitch had anticipated a quiet evening to himself. "Oh, I don't know," he began to protest. "I have an early morning."

"We don't have to stay late. It's barely eight now."

"Suzanne will be bringing the girls home soon," Mitch added.

"Hattie and I can get them ready for bed," Garrett told him with a dismissive wave of his hand. "You kids go have some fun."

Garrett obviously wanted him to get out, so he agreed with little enthusiasm. A night alone sounded much more inviting than a night in a local tavern. Man, he was getting old.

Trina had ridden with Summer, so Collin tossed Mitch the keys to his truck, ensuring Mitch and himself a ride home, then got into Summer's car with her. "See you there!"

Mitch helped Trina into the pickup, getting an eyeful of shapely legs, and climbed in on the driver's side. "Do you feel a little set up here?" he asked, adjusting the mirrors and steering the vehicle down the gravel drive.

"Do you?" she returned.

"A little."

"Do you mind?" she asked.

He glanced over at her curious gaze. She smoothed the red dress over her shapely thighs. "I think my grandfather wants me to meet people so I'll feel like I belong here and want to stay."

They shared a relaxed smile. "Have you been to the Branding Iron before?"

He shook his head.

The interior was dimly lit and smoke-filled. Hundreds of different brands had been burned into the dark wood paneling, the floor, and the bar itself. The center of the room held tables and straight-backed chairs, and hung on the wall behind the bar were mirrors, neon signs and framed photographs of the Crazy Mountains. A few patrons played pool at one end of the low-ceilinged room. A Garth Brooks' song blared from the jukebox in the corner.

Collin flagged them into a booth he'd saved. "What'll you have?" he asked, standing to go get drinks.

Everyone but Summer requested a draft, and she insisted on a Coke. Mitch sipped his beer and joined the conversation, occasionally being introduced to someone new stopping by. Everyone was curious, friendly and accepting.

Trina ate him up with her eyes, openly admiring and inviting, and he was ready to leave after the first fifteen minutes. The whole experience was foreign to Mitch—the dimly lit room, the clink of glasses and bottles, the soft roar of music and voices…the young woman with her hip and thigh pressed invitingly against his, her fingers occasionally touching the inside of his arm.

After the second round, Trina asked him to dance. Mitch exchanged a look with his half brother and, not knowing how to gracefully decline, took the hand she held out. She led him to the dance floor where couples swayed in time to the music in front of the jukebox.

Six

His "date" snuggled into his embrace and hummed along with the slow, sexy Billy Dean song. It had been a long time since Mitch had been in a dating situation. He hadn't seen anyone since his wife's death. Trina smelled of an elusive but expensive scent he couldn't place, nothing as soft or as delicate as the way Heather smelled, but not unpleasant. Her hair felt silky against his chin, and she snuggled her body against his.

The words to the song made him uneasy: words to the effect that he wouldn't be a man if he wasn't affected by a beautiful woman.

Unlike the singer, however, Mitch held back. He was not a man who could live in the moment. He'd have to be dead to not be flattered by Trina's attention—she reminded him of the intoxicating temptation and passion he'd forgotten—but she wasn't the woman the song made him think of.

An alluring picture of a sun-kissed Heather in white shorts and a sexy little sweater formed in his mind.

Trina slid her arms around his neck and pressed her young firm body against his, bringing his attention back to the present. The song changed, and he was grateful for a faster rhythm and the chance to move away from her.

By the time they'd said their good-nights and he'd ridden home with Collin, Mitch was still a little unsure about Garrett's thinking. His life was so uncertain that he wasn't in the market for a love life.

Collin poured himself a glass of milk in the light from the refrigerator.

"You fellas have a good time?" Garrett asked from the doorway. He flipped on the fluorescent overhead light.

"Yeah." Collin blinked. "But I'm beat. Think I'll hit the sack." He polished off his milk and placed the glass in the sink.

"Did you have any problems with the girls?" Mitch asked.

"Nah. Read 'em every book in their case, and they finally gave up."

"Thanks."

"I enjoy them. Nice to have little ones in this house." He placed a cup of water in the microwave and set the timer.

"How about Suzanne? She have any problems?"

"You might want to go over tomorrow to see if Rand needs any help with his septic tank."

Uh-oh. "Why?"

"Oh, they flushed a few things down the toilet. Soap, shampoo, toothpaste—not the bottles and tubes though. Maybe a few pair of Rand's underwear."

Mitch's stomach rolled. His daughters were not exactly a means to make friends and influence people.

"They're just high-spirited," his grandfather said, as if that excused them. "How did you and Trina hit it off?" he asked, dismissing the flushing incident.

Mitch gathered his thoughts. "Just fine."

"She's a cute one, isn't she?"

Mitch nodded.

Garrett stirred a spoonful of instant coffee into his cup. "There are other single young ladies in town. Several of them." He'd picked up on Mitch's lack of enthusiasm.

Mitch studied him curiously. "What is it you're thinking?"

The old man gave him a sheepish smile. "Just that I'd like to see you find someone here and stay. You might find someone you like enough to marry. You'll need a son to pass on the Kincaid land."

Uncomfortable with that suggestion for more than one reason, Mitch remained silent. Mitch would like a wife and perhaps more children—someday, maybe—but he didn't have a problem with leaving any land he inherited to his daughters.

"I appreciate that you want me to stay. I promise I'll give it my full consideration. Dates or no dates."

Garrett sipped his coffee, understanding. "'Night, son."

"'Night." Upstairs, Mitch pulled the sheet up around the sleeping forms of his daughters sharing the double bed, changed into sweatpants and stretched on the narrow daybed. Morning would come quickly. It was a long drive from the ranch to Heather's place, a drive on a winding mountain road that seemed to grow more time-consuming each day. The girls were not easy to get out of bed that early, so this new routine was a challenge—as was everything since his wife died.

There had been an emptiness in his life these past four years, a hollowness that may have been natural, but often made him feel guilty for thinking he needed more than Taylor and Ashley—or that he just needed help with them.

Needing help wasn't a reason to miss his wife—or to think of marrying someone else. He wasn't ready to jump into anything.

He closed his eyes and relaxed.

And into his head came the sight and sounds and smells of the woman who had taken up residence there.

"We're going to finish this back porch this morning," Mitch told Heather the following Monday. "After the carpet's installed this afternoon, we'll move the furniture back into the living room and office. Tomorrow we start on this downstairs bath."

She gave him a thumbs-up. "Sounds like a plan."

She poured the sleepy girls juice and cereal. Her kids weren't up yet. Taylor had arrived cranky and rested her head sullenly on her fist at the table.

"We have to get up an hour earlier to get here in the morning," he explained.

Heather poured him a cup of coffee. "I wondered how hard the drive was on the girls."

"They whine all the way back at night."

"They're young for such a long drive twice every day," she sympathized. She'd considered how to make the situation easier, but nothing short of having the girls stay with her had come to mind. And she wasn't willing to supervise them all night as well as all day. Besides, they needed that time with their father. *She* needed for them to spend that time with their father.

"How about the bunkhouse?" Mitch asked. "Would you consider renting that to me until the ranch is ready to sell?"

Heather had investigated the bunkhouse upon her arrival and knew it to be adequate living space: simple bunks, a functional kitchen with gas and electricity. There was no reason in the world that Mitch shouldn't ease the burden of daily travel and use it.

He would be living and sleeping only yards away. Her late nights had been hers alone for the past several weeks, but she could hardly deny him an arrangement that made things easier for all of them in the long run. "It's probably not very clean."

"Not a problem."

"I wouldn't rent it, but you're welcome to use it, if you're sure you want to."

"I am. All we need is a place to sleep at night."

And she would have to think of him sleeping over there at night. "I'll take the kids over with me and do some cleaning this morning," she said, then turned when she remembered something she'd wanted to ask. "If I go buy a swing set and sandbox, will you help me put them together?"

A smile lifted one side of his mouth. "You going to take them back apart and move them to California with you?"

"No, I'll just leave them or sell them."

"Then I'll help you—if you let me pay for half."

The playground equipment would entertain his children as well as hers. "Deal."

He gave his daughters the usual subtle warnings to behave themselves and headed out the screen door. Heather watched him take a tool belt from the lock box on the back of the borrowed pickup and buckle it around his narrow hips. He looked as sexy in his work clothes as she'd imagined he would that first day. He smacked a cap against his thigh and adjusted it on his head in a charmingly masculine gesture.

She stood at the screen door a little longer than necessary, admiring the morning sun on his sandy hair, the play of muscles beneath the thin fabric of his T-shirt as he carried his toolboxes to the house. And now he'd be close by 'round the clock.

She turned and busied herself. A few minutes later when his workers arrived, Heather carried a thermos of coffee out to them.

Jessica, who had awakened by the time she returned to the kitchen, carried a pajama-clad Andrew on her hip. Patrick followed a short time later, and her day was under way.

She assigned the older children tasks in the bunkhouse, and they took turns keeping an eye on Andrew. Taylor seemed a little more comfortable with her today, even joining in the tasks without complaint. By lunchtime, everything was finished except the last loads of sheets and blankets to wash.

After lunch, Heather selected audio tapes for the stereo in the Blazer, packed snacks and books, and headed for Billings to purchase the outside toys. The children slept most of the way home, which was good, because she was concerned about the boxes tied to the top of the vehicle. She kept an eye on the road behind her and an ear peeled for disaster.

Mitch met her as she turned off the engine.

"I couldn't get the sandbox," she told him. "It was too big."

"I get my truck back tomorrow," he said, his eyes bright blue in the shade of his cap. "I'll go get it."

He untied the boxes that the dock workers had efficiently tied to the roof, and Ronnie, one of his crew, helped him lower them to the ground. The kids roused and filed out.

"I thought this plastic set would be quicker to put together than one of the wooden jobs," she told him.

"Probably," he said with a shrug. "Come on in and see the carpet."

The back porch had been roofed and painted, a

white railing constructed around the entire perimeter. "This looks great!"

She followed him into the house and admired the carpet. "It makes the rooms look so much bigger—and homier," she said, pleased with the outcome. The men had put the furnishings back into place. "But it sure makes this dirty old furniture look tacky."

Mitch shrugged. "That's for the new owners to deal with."

She tried to imagine new owners placing their furniture on the carpet she'd selected, hanging curtains on the clean windows and pictures on the newly painted walls. She cast the harmfully proprietary thought aside. "The bunkhouse is clean. How soon do you want to move in?"

"I'll bring our things tomorrow. Wanna get that swing set together?"

"Sure. We can do it after supper."

He nodded. "I'll call Garrett and let him know I won't be there."

Heather quickly prepared a salad and spaghetti. Mitch was in and out of the house, stopping once to use the phone. She heard him ask for his grandfather. "I'm staying at the Bolton place for supper.... Oh. Did she leave a message? I'll call her later, or maybe not until tomorrow, depending on what time I get in tonight. I do want to talk to you, though. Okay. Later."

Mitch stood staring at his hand on the phone after he'd hung it up.

"Everything okay?" she asked.

"Oh—yeah, fine."

"Supper's ready."

"I'll call the kids and wash up."

Once seated at the big round oak table, Heather dished up portions and served them to the children.

"I don't like this kind of spaghetti," Taylor said immediately.

Heather's heart sank just a little. For Mitch.

"Eat a little anyway," he coaxed. "Heather went to a lot of trouble to fix it for us."

"Will you buy me ice cream on the way home if I eat some bites?" she asked.

Mitch glanced at Heather, then at her children, who were already digging into their meal. She met his eyes and read his confusion. She didn't want to intrude and make him angry, but the girls were now saving their manipulations for their father. They'd come to terms with her and her rules, but they still knew which of their father's buttons to push.

"Excuse us for one minute," Mitch said to the children. He stood and took Heather's arm, guiding her into the adjoining dining room. The feel of his callused fingers against her bare skin clouded Heather's thoughts. A shiver ran up her spine.

She glanced up into his eyes. An unspoken recognition passed between them, startling her. He felt something when he touched her, just as she did when he was close. The electricity was there, beneath the surface, a consuming energy that wouldn't flare if they didn't acknowledge it.

He released her arm and she focused on his face.

"Do you deal with this every meal?" he asked, his brow crinkling.

She shook her head, ignoring the shape of his mobile mouth. "We're past this. They eat fine for me. Truly."

"Then why?" he asked, puzzlement and confusion plain in his concerned eyes. He ran a hand through his freshly washed hair, and her fingertips tingled.

She felt his frustration all the way to her toes. Her heart softened even more toward him. "Because they have to test you. They've pushed you this far and they'll continue to push you until you put your foot down once and for all."

"What do I do?"

"Tell them they don't have to eat anything they don't want to. Pretty soon they'll get hungry enough to eat what you place in front of them. And pretty soon they'll like it."

"But they need to eat something."

"Breakfast isn't that far away. When Taylor gets hungry, she'll eat, no matter what's placed in front of her."

"Those tantrums she throws—"

"The tantrums have lessened, too," she said, placing a hand on his forearm without considering the reaction she would have to touching him. It was immediate and disturbing. Her every sense zeroed in on the place where their skin met. She withdrew her hand away quickly. "I think they feel silly in front of the other kids. You're the one they want to manipulate." She didn't want to hurt him, but honesty was best.

He stood, lost in thought for a moment, and she understood how difficult it must be to accept her advice.

"All right. I've seen your methods work where nothing I've done has, so I'll take my cues from you." They exchanged another look, then he turned back toward the kitchen.

Heather served Mitch and herself and sat.

Mitch took a deep breath to prepare. "You don't have to eat the spaghetti if you don't like it."

Taylor glanced from her father to Heather. "Will you get me something else?"

Heather gave Mitch a slight negative shake of her head.

"No," he said.

The child thrust her lower lip out, and shot Heather a dark look before asking her father, "Will you get me ice cream on the way home?"

Heather didn't even look at Mitch this time. He was on his own.

He didn't even look at Heather. "No. If you don't like the spaghetti, you don't get anything."

"But I'm hungry!"

"The salad is good," Patrick said, obviously trying to humor Taylor and make peace in his own five-year-old way.

"The bread's good, too," Ashley added, and Mitch almost fell off his chair. Ashley was attempting to get her sister to eat?

He waited for Taylor to do something outrageous and embarrassing, but she only glanced at the other kids at the table and crossed her arms over her chest with a pout.

When she thought no one was looking, Taylor took a bite of bread or selected a few vegetables from her salad bowl. She never did touch the spaghetti, but Mitch felt an enormous victory had been won here tonight.

He thought of all the times he'd stressed and worried over them not eating. A week under Heather's direction and their mealtime disorder had been set to rights. He felt doubly foolish for allowing the situation to have grown so out of control and grateful to Heather for handling it so well.

"Thank you," he said to her later as he wiped sauce from the floor beneath the wooden high chair. He straightened and carried the dishrag to the sink.

"For what?" she asked, not turning away from the plates she was rinsing.

"For knowing what to do and for being firm—with all of us."

"I kept thinking about what you said," she told him. "About feeling sorry for them for not having a mother, and I understood, only to a small degree, what you must be feeling." She turned off the water and dried her hands. "I have spells where I feel guilty for taking the kids away from their father. I want to make it up to them. But of course I can't.''

A personal revelation. The first she'd ever made. Mitch held his breath, waiting for more.

Seven

"And it's different in my situation," she went on, "because I was always their main caregiver and the disciplinarian. Their father didn't have much to do with them, really. But I think a child needs a father."

She glanced at him, and he concentrated on her words, not on the fact that she'd shared something intimate about her life. She'd never opened up the least bit with him, especially about her marriage, and the slowly developing trust her words showed touched him deeply. He simply nodded.

"With Taylor and Ashley, it was their mother that they lost," she went on. "I can only assume she was a good mother and that the majority of their time was with her while you worked."

"She was a terrific mother," Mitch said, eager now to share more. "Even though we were totally blown away by having twins, she took it in stride. We bought one of those double strollers and she took them for walks. She never got enough sleep at night, but I didn't hear her complain. She always seemed to have enough time and energy and love for both of them." He dropped his gaze and watched Heather's hands as she folded the towel. "And for me."

Talk about personal. That last part had slipped out without thought. He turned and leaned against the sink, looking away from her sympathetic expression, but the words wouldn't stop. "It was frightening when she got sick. I didn't know what to do. Not for her. Not for them. And when she died...the whole world got knocked off kilter."

She was silent for a few minutes. The sound of the television drifted from the other room. He felt as though he'd exposed too much of his private emotions, but because he'd never really said as much to anyone before, it was almost a relief that he could finally express his confusion. Somehow he knew this woman understood and didn't think less of him.

"You love them, Mitch, and that's all that really matters." Her low voice held compassion. "Because you're doing the very best you know how."

She even understood. Oh, Lord, she understood. "I just wish I knew how better."

"We all have a lot to learn."

He turned his head and looked over at her where she stood leaning against the sink, her eyes filled with warmth and understanding. She was lovely and desirable, the kind of woman any man would love to make his own. He wondered for the first time what kind of man her husband had been.

"Why did you leave your husband?" he asked, the question leaving his lips before he could think better of it. "What went wrong?"

Her expression shuttered abruptly. "Things were wrong all along."

He waited, hoping she'd say more, hoping he hadn't ruined their tentative familiarity. But she pushed away from the sink and took the stack of plates he'd dried and placed them in the cupboard.

"Did you love him?" The question was entirely personal. Not at all what he would normally consider asking, but their conversation had turned intimate, at least for him, and it seemed the right thing to wonder.

"I loved everything that he represented," she said finally.

"Which was?"

"Determination. Discipline." She hesitated. "Freedom."

What an odd thing to say. "Freedom from what?"

Closing the cupboard, she glanced around. "Let's get started on that swing set."

Her obvious rebuff hurt. He'd trusted her enough to bare his soul, yet she refused to share anything too personal. He'd offered her information freely, he realized; she'd never asked questions, but she'd listened with compassion. He didn't want her sympathy, and he didn't like the feeling that she saw right into the core of him, but didn't want him to pry.

They carried the boxes with the parts, and Mitch retrieved a toolbox. The children waited impatiently, finally running toward the barn in pursuit of a cat.

Heather read the instructions, but Mitch followed his own impulsive plan, finally admitting he didn't know what some of the screws and bolts were for. She held the plastic tubing and made suggestions while he placed and tightened the screws.

It was dusk when he pronounced the gym set child-safe. The kids shrieked and clambered for the swings and slide. Heather gave a lesson on taking turns and not pushing, while Mitch chased Andrew who wanted to go back to the barn. The little boy had grown tired and cried when Mitch picked him up and carried him back.

"He's just sleepy," Heather said, pushing Taylor and Patrick in the swings. Jessica and Ashley were team sliding on the plastic slide.

Mitch carried the two-year-old to the porch where they could watch the others play. He sat in the creaky wicker rocker, with the boy in his lap, his head nestled in the crook of his arm, and remembered the sweetness of his own babies when they were this young. Andrew gave him a few bashful looks from beneath heavy eyelids, and then gradually fell into exhausted slumber.

Heather led the rest of the children across the porch and into the kitchen.

"Shall I take him upstairs?" Mitch asked.

She nodded, sat the others at the table and poured them drinks, then followed. She led him into a bedroom and pulled back the covers on a double bed. "He sleeps in here," she said softly. Lifting him over the side guard, Mitch lowered him to the mattress.

Heather put a diaper on him, covered him with the

sheet, then smoothed his hair back from his forehead.
Seeing Mitch with him had had a disturbing effect on
her chest. The same strong hands that swung a hammer and fitted planks of wood were gentle and caring
when they touched her baby.

The thought of them touching her made her nerve
endings tremble. She turned and straightened, unex-
pectedly moving right against Mitch who'd been
standing close. Those hands closed over her upper
arms, and he steadied her. She had to close her eyes
to fight the dizziness.

"Oh," she said, a soft sound of surprise. She
opened one hand against his warm knit-covered chest
to balance herself, and beneath her fingers, his heart
beat steadily.

Mitch's body responded immediately to the sensory
attack. She smelled like dish soap and outdoors, with
an alluring feminine scent all her own underneath.
Her golden-brown eyes held a question...and an invitation.

As if it had a mind of its own, his hand raised to
caress a strand of silky hair. He smoothed a tress between his fingers and thumb, tucked it behind her ear
as he'd seen her do, then ran a finger across her ivory
cheek.

Her eyes darkened and the pulse at her throat raced
visibly.

He couldn't help himself. He lowered his head and
touched her lips with his own.

Her quickly drawn breath was either surprise or

pleasure, and he hoped it was the latter. Her mouth was warm and soft, and she leaned into the kiss as though hungry for his taste.

Mitch released her arm and braced her shoulder with his forearm, placing both hands in the hair that he'd wanted to feel and threading his fingers into the cool silkiness.

She was incredibly soft, her body pliant and her lips eager. He could lose himself in this woman in a heartbeat.

Starved for her now, sensing the sharp promise of pleasure, he opened his mouth over hers. At the first touch of his tongue against her lips, she made a provocative sound and grasped his T-shirt in her fist.

Their lips parted slightly, enough to breathe, enough to still taste, and he sought her again with his tongue. She met his fervent quest with the tip of her tongue, teasing him, testing him, until he felt her body quake.

She leaned away and opened her eyes to meet his. He saw fire…and uncertainty…and unspoken need.

She composed her expression, took a breath and let go of his shirt. At her withdrawal, Mitch automatically released her and let his hands fall to his sides. The sense of loss was devastating.

"Heather," he whispered.

She shook her head and brought the backs of her fingers to her flaming cheek. "No," she said, her voice trembling. "Don't say anything." She raised both hands as though warding him off. "Please, don't say anything."

Obediently silent, he turned and left the room, his mind and his body screaming for her. Downstairs the children had finished their drinks and were sitting outside on the porch in the dark.

"Let's go, girls," he said softly.

Tired, they followed and buckled themselves into their seat belts. Mitch checked them, then turned and waved at Jessica and Patrick. "See you in the morning."

Illuminated by the light from the kitchen window, they returned the wave. Heather appeared, a slender silhouette in the doorway.

Mitch placed the truck in gear and drove down the gravel drive, trying to make sense of what had happened. She had awakened him to the demands and desires of his body, and now he couldn't shut them off. Didn't know if he wanted to. Heather had started out as a job, but she'd quickly become a friend. He didn't want to do anything to ruin either one of those.

If he had offended her, he needed to apologize, but she hadn't allowed him to speak. He didn't know what he would have said, anyway—probably something stupid. Probably something completely out of line that he'd have been sorry for later. Like the kiss.

Like the kiss.

Was he sorry for that kiss?

Blessedly, the girls had fallen asleep and he had his thoughts to himself on the long ride home. Tomorrow he'd be moving even closer to Heather Johnson. He'd better get a grip on his agitated hormones right away.

Heather sat on the back porch in the dark and watched the fireflies dance in the cattails along the edge of the pond. What had happened to her?

What was it about this place that made people crazy? She'd found herself constantly looking at Mitch Fielding with preposterously sexy thoughts. She'd never mused in that feverish manner before—not about any man in particular anyway. She'd had fantasies, of course—inconsequential daydreams of some faceless lover—but she'd never looked at a man and reacted the way she reacted to this man.

It must be this place. She needed to get out of here. She needed to get the project finished, sell the damned ranch and return to her normal existence.

Getting up, she locked the doors and made her way upstairs, where she ran a bubble bath in the deep claw-foot tub.

Heather sank down into the scented water. She would tell Mitch this tub had to stay.

Remembering the way his simple touch on her arm set her skin tingling, she closed her eyes, leaned back, and relished the memories. The strength of her reactions frightened her. Looking at him made her soft and wet inside. Smelling him…her chest fluttered… She was like some primitive animal drawn to the scent of another, she thought with self-deprecation. His nearness was tantalizing. His scent provocative.

She was the almost-thirty-year-old mother of three children. She'd been married for nearly ten years. She had never had these overpowering feelings toward a man before.

She'd felt distaste, disgust, fear, warmth from time to time, grudging respect, but never this—this attraction. This *craving*.

Her body remembered his touch. His kiss. The intoxicating loss of control and the frantic desire to possess, be possessed. The memory excited and embarrassed her even now.

Her head knew better.

But Heather had the feeling that she wouldn't give a second thought to what her head was telling her if the opportunity arose again. That lack of restraint terrified her.

And thrilled her.

Snared in a new web of sensuality, she ran more hot water and rethought her hesitation and the reasons behind it.

She had begun a new life, a life of independence. She was in control of her own body and making her own decisions. She could choose to enjoy herself and explore her sexuality if she wanted to. She was her own person. And she could choose to keep her head in control and not be pushed into a commitment she wanted no part of. No longer was she a foolish young girl in need of a rescuer.

She wanted to find out what this attraction for Mitch was all about. The way he made her feel was an intoxicant she had to explore and wanted to experience. She sank deeper into the scented water and allowed her mind to wander where it would. Exactly how much courage did she really possess?

Eight

Finding his grandfather in the study, Mitch rapped his knuckles on the open door as he entered. "How did the meeting go with Jordan Baxter?"

Disgust clouded Garrett's normally pleasant expression. "Damn pigheaded fool is what that man is. He refuses to listen to reason."

"I take it you didn't come to an agreement."

"The only thing we came close to was blows. I'm not the most even-tempered when I get around him, either, so I might have figured we'd need a referee."

"So the court date's still set."

"If he won't listen to me, I guess he'll be forced to answer to the judge."

"I hope the ruling turns out the way you want it to."

"How's the work going?" Garrett asked, changing the subject.

Mitch outlined the day's accomplishments, pleased that Garrett took such an interest. "The girls and I are going to stay in Heather's bunkhouse until the work is done," he explained. "The drive twice a day is getting to all of us. The morning that it rained, I was uncomfortable about having them on those mountain roads in that weather.''

"I can understand that thinking," Garrett replied. "But isn't there some other way around it?"

"I was lucky to get Heather to watch them during the day," Mitch reminded him.

"You could work here, on the ranch," the old man suggested, not for the first time.

"I'd still need someone to take care of them. And I know you don't really need another hand right now. I don't want to feel like I'm a charity case. I'm perfectly capable of supporting myself and my girls."

"I know you are. It's not that. It's just that... I guess I'll miss havin' you around. I've made it plain enough that I'd like you to stay here—on the ranch— in Whitehorn, for good. Have you thought about it?"

"Sure, I have." Mitch sat in a chair across from him. "Getting to know Collin and Cade and all of my half brothers is important to me. I want to know all of them better. I feel like I belong here, like I belong with them—and with you—more than I ever did with my stepfather and stepbrother and sisters. Not because of anything anyone ever said or did," he added quickly.

"Just because I never felt like I belonged with them. I was always an outsider. They loved me and accepted me, but I was always a reminder, even if it was only in my own mind, of my mother's premarital affair." He laughed wryly. "Here, I'm just one of the many."

"No one thinks any less of you because of your father's philandering," Garrett told him.

"I know. And it's crazy, because even though everyone in town knows about my parentage, it doesn't matter."

"So you're leanin' toward stayin'?"

"I can't say yet. I would never want to hurt my mother. The girls are doing better away from her and their other grandmother, though."

"I won't rush you," Garrett promised. "But while you're stayin' at the Bolton place, you'll come to dinner on the weekends?"

"We will."

"And the girls can stay with me and Hattie while you get out and make friends."

Mitch accepted the suggestion good-naturedly. "Okay."

Garrett got to his feet when Mitch did. He stepped forward and gave his grandson an awkward hug.

Though it was a little after ten, Mitch returned Trina's call from the phone on the kitchen wall. "Were you sleeping?"

"Oh, no," she replied. "I'm a night owl."

"I got your message."

"I was wondering if you wanted to drive into Billings with me Saturday night. We could see a movie, have dinner or something."

He'd just been asked out. On a date. He thought about the last time he'd seen her, the way he'd really wanted nothing more than to have the night over with.

"I'm really flattered..." he began.

"But?" she interrupted.

"But I wouldn't want to mislead you."

"And you can't see us going anywhere."

"Sorry."

"Hey, a girl can appreciate honesty."

"I'll be seeing you around," he said lamely.

"Sure. Take care, then. Maybe some other time."

Mitch knew there wouldn't be another time. Especially not after what had happened with Heather earlier. If there was anyone in Whitehorn he wanted to get to know better, it was the lovely young mother of three who had gotten under his skin without trying.

The next morning Mitch had extra driving to do. He picked up his repaired and cleaned truck, and drove back to his grandfather's ranch. The girls were playing in the yard beside the house and ran to meet him. "You got our truck fixed!"

He knelt to give them each a hug. "Yes, I did. And I know two young ladies who need to say they're sorry for costing me so much trouble and money."

"I'm sorry, Daddy," Ashley said immediately. She threw her arms around his neck again.

"I'm sorry," Taylor said finally, stubbing her toe in the dirt.

"All right. I forgive you both. But I never ever want you to play in a car or truck again. Understand? One of you could have been hurt very badly. Or one of the other kids could have been hurt."

Taylor didn't talk back, but she dragged her feet the whole time they were packing and getting their things ready to go. She obviously wasn't taking well to his new decisiveness.

Mitch secured boxes of toys in the back of the pickup and stacked their clothing and personal items inside the crew cab. It was much like coming to Montana from Minnesota had been, and he realized then that he was going to have to make a permanent decision about their home soon, for the girls's sakes. School would be starting and he would need to have them settled.

It was midmorning when they arrived at Heather's place. The crew had been at work tearing out the downstairs wall for the new combination laundry room and bath.

He simply backed the truck up to the bunkhouse and left the unloading for later. He escorted the girls to where Heather was playing with her kids on the swings.

"Morning," she said, smiling cheerfully at the twins.

Ashley surprised Mitch by giving Heather an impulsive hug before joining the others.

"I'm late," Mitch told her. "I'd better get to work."

He joined his workers in shoveling the heavy plaster and insulation into the trash container that had been delivered. By late afternoon the wall was gone and the debris cleared away. Mitch measured, strung off the section for a foundation to be poured, and recalculated how much concrete he'd need.

"Are you going to eat?" Heather called to him after his men had gone home for the day.

"This has to be finished by tonight," he replied. "Concrete's coming in the morning."

"Come eat some supper."

"Ten minutes," he said.

A half hour later he showed up at the back door, sweaty, his body aching. "Can I have a plate out here?"

"You think I never smelled a hardworking man before?" She carried a plate and a glass of milk. Her impish smile assured him she was having fun with him.

"Have you?" he asked, her friendly manner an encouragement he hadn't hoped for.

"Sure. I grew up on this ranch, remember?"

"I guess I hadn't thought about it." He sat on the top step, placed the plate on the porch floor, and dug into the steak she'd grilled to medium-rare perfection. "Did my girls eat steak?"

"No, they had skettios."

He grinned. "Watch it, they'll want to stay here forever. What are they doing now?"

"Why? The silence got you scared?"

He shot her a comical glance, relaxing even more. "Yeah."

She laughed. "They're putting puzzles together. Andrew is eating the pieces."

"Do you want to talk about last night yet?"

"No."

He studied her delicate profile, noted the pink that touched her cheeks. "Why not?"

"Because I don't know what to say, and I don't want to spoil it by analyzing it. If you're trying to get me to comment or apologize or something, it's not going to work."

"I'll take that to mean you're not sorry." At her raised brow, he waved a hand, then gestured to his plate. "Never mind. This is incredible."

"Thank you. We worked on the bunkhouse again this afternoon, so you don't have to worry about that this evening."

He glanced up in surprise. "You mean, you put our things away?"

"We did."

"Man, you are efficient."

"That's me. Efficient."

Mitch finished his meal and she took the plate back to the kitchen. Collecting his daughters, he escorted them to the bunkhouse.

Heather had not only cleaned, she'd added throw rugs to the scarred wooden floor and made up three beds with crisp sheets and comfortable quilts. All their clothing had been hung or placed in drawers, and Taylor's and Ashley's toys were neatly stored, their favorite dolls and stuffed animals lining their beds.

The refrigerator held a supply of milk and juice,

and a can of coffee stood beside the percolator. She'd thought of everything and handled it competently, as usual.

Mitch had read the girls a book, then tucked them into their bunks and sat with them until they'd fallen asleep. Now, he leaned against the porch rail and studied the mountain peaks in the moonlight. The lights in the big house went out one by one, and then the screen door squeaked.

She'd be sitting on the porch if he wandered over. He moved to the first step. But he wouldn't. He didn't want to take advantage of her friendship. In the darkness, he turned, found a wooden rocker and lowered his weight onto the seat. He didn't want to risk making a fool of himself again by coming on to her, and her nearness had a profound effect on him.

He'd expected her to treat him coolly after her reaction last night, so her friendliness and matter-of-fact statement that she didn't want to analyze their kiss gave him hope.

He hadn't felt anything resembling hope in a long time. Mitch set the rocker in motion and enjoyed the feeling.

Nine

Heather slathered more sunscreen on Andrew and helped him back into the inflatable pool where she sat enjoying the cool water. Mitch had not only picked up and painstakingly filled the sandbox the day before, but he'd also purchased, inflated, and filled a pool. He'd even thought to buy swim toys for all the children as well as a supply of sunscreen.

He'd taken the girls to Garrett's for Sunday dinner today, but before he'd left, he'd spent an hour in the sandbox, bulldozing sand roads with Patrick and Andrew.

He was a wonderful father. He'd had some problems disciplining Taylor and Ashley, yes, but he was working on that. It was obvious that he desired what was best for them and that he worked hard to give them a fulfilling childhood and a loving environment. The comparison to her father was as different as night and day.

Pete Bolton had lost himself in the oblivion of alcohol and left the care of his only child to a bitter old woman who demanded perfection and punished anything less with physical violence and isolation.

Heather had tried to bury her tragic childhood and

hadn't wanted to resurrect it. Coming to Montana—
to this ranch—had unearthed the painful memories.
She watched Jessica, so young and beautiful, spar-
kling with life and vitality, playing with her brothers
and thought of herself at ten—silent, resentful, locked
away for hours and hours without human contact,
without love.

Feeling sorry for herself changed nothing. That was
why she'd never wanted to come here, never wanted
to be reminded. She'd put this behind her and moved
forward.

But it was good that she'd come, she realized now.
She hadn't been as ruthless as that hateful housekeeper, but she'd found herself with some of the same
rigid ideals and expectations. She never wanted her
children to believe perfection was the only acceptable
standard, and Mitch had showed her how to give a
little slack—with her children and with herself.

She wasn't perfect. Far from it.

"Watch this, Mommy!"

Heather laughed at Patrick's antics in the water and
splashed him back. She was glad that when the kids
had asked her to join them in the pool, she'd decided
flexibility could be fun.

Without conscious decision, she compared Mitch
to her former husband, and sadly wondered why, of
all the young men she could have chosen to help her
escape, she had latched on to another emotional re-
cluse. Craig had wanted to control her, but he'd never
shared himself with her. Since Heather had no posi-

tive example, it had taken years for her to recognize how warped their marriage had been.

Months of counseling had helped her get past her own guilt and prevent her from carrying any of the baggage of her childhood or marriage into her relationship with her children. She loved them above all else and had determined to show them unconditional love and acceptance.

Sometimes her own strict disciplinary tendencies frightened her, but she had learned that discipline with love didn't stem from a desire to control or hurt. Getting away from Craig was the best thing she'd ever done for herself—and for her children.

The Silverado appeared on the long drive, and she watched the shiny vehicle coming closer. Patrick noticed the truck and, in his exuberance, plunged head-first over the side of the pool landing on the grass.

Mitch parked and stepped out, splendidly handsome in black jeans and boots, a dark red shirt accentuating his tan and sun-bleached hair. An odd catch tugged at Heather's heart.

"Hey, buddy!" he said to Patrick, ruffling his wet hair.

"Come watch me be a shark," Patrick said.

"Me a shark!" Andrew called, and Heather caught him as he tripped and fell forward into the water.

"Can we swim, Daddy?" Taylor begged, tugging on her father's arm.

The Fielding trio walked closer. Heather shaded her eyes to look up from her seat in the shallow water.

She couldn't see him well with the bright sunlight behind him, until his shadow fell over her, blocking the sun so she could peer up.

Her one-piece suit was as modest as they came, so she didn't know why she suddenly felt embarrassed at his perusal.

"Can we get in, Daddy?" Ashley asked.

"Sure. Go get your suits on."

They squealed and ran toward the bunkhouse. Jessica climbed out and followed.

"Watch, Mitch!" Patrick called. He lay on his tummy in the water, one hand projecting from his head like a fin, and went under.

"Looks like a shark to me," Mitch told him.

"Watch me!" Andrew mimicked, and fell face forward, intentionally this time. Heather helped him regain his balance.

"You're a good shark, too," he laughingly told Andrew.

The girls returned and splashed so much, Mitch had to get the hose to refill the pool. He toed off his boots and placed them and his shirt on the back porch, well away from the play area.

Taylor shrieked as a stream of cold water from the hose hit her, then jumped out of the pool. "Squirt me, Daddy!"

He obliged her and it turned into a new game until the others joined them, the grass becoming so slick and muddy that they all slipped and slid.

Heather found a towel and wrapped it around her hips as she watched the antics.

"Me a shark!"

She heard the tiny voice at the same time Mitch turned toward the pool, and her heart did a flip in her chest. Running the few feet, she saw Andrew climb over the side and hit the water face-first with a splash.

Heather's feet slipped in the slick grass, and she lost her balance. By the time she righted herself, Mitch had reached the pool. Heather smacked into him and he caught her around the waist.

Andrew had regained his own footing and stood by himself, his face wreathed in a grin, showing off his pearly white teeth.

"Andrew Mitchell Johnson, don't you *ever* swim by yourself again," she admonished. "You wait for Mommy."

His grin faded and he puckered up for a cry.

Heather became aware of Mitch's hand on her wet suit and the warm, damp skin of his bare side along her arm.

She placed one foot in the pool to pick up Andrew, and Mitch helped her back over onto the grass, still gently guiding her, his hand around her shoulder. "He's all right," he said softly. "We were both right here."

She nodded.

"I'll drain the pool every evening," he promised.

She was reluctant for him to move away, to release his comforting hold. His skin smelled warm and salty, like sun and man and…pleasure. She really hadn't been all that frightened. She'd seen that Mitch was there ahead of her, and she knew Andrew could stand in the shallow water. Her urgency to reach him had been one of those gut-instinct reactions.

"Let's dry off and get dressed," she said to the kids who had gathered around them. Mitch released her and they stepped apart. "Taylor and Ashley, would you like to join us for popcorn and a movie?"

"Yes, please!" Ashley said with a vigorous nod.

"What's the movie?" Taylor asked.

"*Annie,*" Jessica supplied.

"You'll like it," Patrick predicted. "Mrs. Hannigan is real mean, and Annie gets a 'dopted new dad and mom."

Later, with the house smelling of popcorn, Heather and Mitch sat at opposite ends of the sofa. Throughout the movie, one or more children were either between them or on their laps.

Heather popped more popcorn, wiped up juice and refilled Andrew's sippy cup. He fell asleep with his head in her lap while she smoothed his dark hair with her fingers.

Glancing over, she caught the hot look in Mitch's eyes as he studied her. Warmth spread throughout her body. Theirs was the most innocent of situations. Ashley sat on Mitch's lap, her blond ponytail brushing his chin. Nothing had been said or done to create the aura of sensual friction that arced between them.

Completely uncomfortable with the disquiet, she

excused herself to take her son up to his bed. She diapered and covered him before she returned. Ashley had moved to her stomach on the newly carpeted floor between her sister and Patrick. Jessica sat in a rocker, idly brushing a doll's hair as she watched the movie.

The sad-sweet comparison that loomed in Heather's thoughts carved an ache in her chest. They looked like a family here in this house, sharing the evening and doing normal, ordinary things. She couldn't remember one time that Craig had ever lounged on the sofa of their expensively furnished and decorated family room and shared a movie or a bowl of popcorn with his own children.

Heather headed for the kitchen to wash bowls and plastic cups. Mitch carried a bowl with old maids in the bottom and placed it on the counter. His gaze burned into her back as she washed and rinsed the bowl.

"Is there any chance," he asked, his voice low, "that you might not go back to San Francisco?"

Struggling to focus on her task, Heather turned off the water and dried her hands. She understood what he was asking. He was asking if there was any chance for them—a possibility that they might explore this odd, exhilarating tension to see what could develop. Her heart leaped with the possibility. But she knew it was only fair to extinguish any thoughts of something more permanent.

"I have a job there. A life. I'm going back." She turned, ashamed of the tremor in her voice, and stoked her courage to meet his eyes. "This place isn't for me."

Mitch had needed to ask, had needed to test the waters to see if by some remote chance, she was feeling something for him in return. There was an attraction, of course, a pull between them. But it must be nothing she couldn't ignore to get back to her preferable, more desirable life.

Neither of them had done or said anything that evening that would lead one to think that there was more going on than met the eye. But under the surface, an entirely different communication hummed in eloquent silence.

He'd known what she would say. Imagining the two of them together was unrealistic. She'd said it all—she had a life to return to, one she apparently enjoyed very much.

He wished he knew exactly what he wanted as certainly as she did.

Her lovely golden eyes were still studying him, and for the first time he thought he read regret in their depths. She seemed so self-assured and confident, but was she really having doubts? Second thoughts? Desires? Would it be unfair of him to try to tip the scales in his favor?

Maybe he was a dreamer. Maybe his hopes were unfounded. Maybe this thing between them wouldn't even amount to anything when put to the test. Some things were better in fantasy than reality.

"Okay," he said finally, moving aside so she could

place the bowls in the cupboard. He probably imagined the breath she released.

When the movie ended, Mitch herded the twins off to their quarters. Tomorrow was Monday and he needed his rest.

But sleep evaded him.

He kept thinking about the irony of his situation, and the more he thought about it, the more confused he became. Trina was an attractive, available young woman who wanted things to develop between them while he shared no similar interest.

Heather was a beautiful *un*available woman who stirred his blood and verbally put the brakes on any ideas he might have of developing a relationship. ''Verbally'' was the key there. Physically, she responded to him. And that was the hope that kept him awake all night.

Ten

Heather kept her promise to Jessica and called the nearby rancher who had been boarding her father's horses. Then she inspected the saddles and tack and found them in surprisingly good condition.

After supper on Tuesday, she approached Mitch as he straightened tools in the lockbox on the back of his truck. The children were playing on the swings and in the sandbox.

"I have a favor to ask," she said, looking up to where he stood in the bed of the truck.

He dropped what he was doing and leaned on the side to give her his attention. His hair and clothing were powdered with drywall dust. "Sure."

"I was wondering if I could ask you to watch the boys for me for a few hours sometime this weekend. I'd like to take Jessica riding."

"No problem. Name the time."

"I don't want to interfere with your plans."

"I haven't made any yet. I want to work Saturday morning, and Sunday I'll have dinner with Garrett. So any other time is fine."

"Sunday morning?" she asked. "Would that work?"

"That'd be fine."

"It's not asking too much?"

"Heather, you take care of my girls for me all the time. The least I can do is return the favor once."

"But that's different. It's part of our deal."

"You don't treat them like a business deal," he said softly. "You're the best thing that's happened to them in a long time."

His praise embarrassed her, and she glanced aside. "They've come a long way," she said, giving them the credit.

"I'm honored you're trusting me with *your* children," he said with a teasing grin.

"Just don't ruin years of training while I'm out riding." Her reply didn't hold the least bit of true concern.

"I might turn them into chauvinists before you get back."

"You? Ha!" She'd never met a man with less chauvinistic tendencies than this one. He helped with dishes, kissed skinned knees, bathed children, wiped up spaghetti sauce, and interpreted baby talk like no other. If her husband had shared half of this man's qualities, she'd still be married to him.

The revealing thought shocked her.

He grinned down at her, and something warm and liquid spread throughout her body. Her heart beat faster. She wondered then what his wife had been like, if she'd known what an incredible father he would be to her children, if she'd appreciated him.

This was crazy thinking. Heather arrested her thoughts immediately and backed away from the truck. "Thank you. It means a lot to Jessica—and to me."

"No problem." His smile faded. She hurried toward where the children played.

After Mitch had finished sorting his tools and checking supplies for tomorrow's work, he showered and joined Heather on the back porch.

She was rocking Andrew to sleep, while Jessica read a book and the other kids quietly played a board game at Heather's feet.

"You've made incredible progress this week," she said, referring to the framing and drywall in the new addition.

"Did as much as I could myself," he said. "I could have done the electricity, too, but I didn't want any questions when it's inspected for a new loan."

"I have flooring picked out," she said. "Do you want it delivered?"

"I'll send one of the guys to pick it up," he replied.

"It was my turn," Ashley said to her sister, and Mitch turned toward the squabble. "You took the wrong turn."

"Did not," Taylor denied.

Ashley plaintively looked up at her father.

"Taylor, is it possible you just made a mistake and moved out of turn?"

"Maybe," she said with a pout. She sat up and moved away, crossing her arms over her chest.

Mitch moved to sit beside her. "I sure have been proud of you lately," he said.

She turned blue eyes up to her father.

"You've been acting so grown up and not throwing temper tantrums like little kids do. I've even noticed how you share with the others."

Taylor's arms dropped to her sides.

"I been good, too, Daddy," Ashley said.

"Yes, you have."

Ashley moved over and climbed into her father's lap for a hug.

Taylor observed the two of them, but didn't move toward her father. Heather had noticed more than once how Mitch and Ashley often hugged and held hands, and how Taylor hung back.

He wasn't unaware, however. Once Ashley had scooted back over to the board game, Mitch tapped Taylor's nose with his index finger, and she grinned up at him. He leaned over and kissed the top of her head. The sight gave Heather a lump in her throat.

"Mom, can Taylor and Ashley sleep over with me tonight?" Jessica asked, looking up from her book. Heather knew she was missing her friends from California, and sleepovers were one of their favorite activities.

"If they want to and it's all right with their dad," she replied.

"Do you guys want to?" Jess asked. "We can use my glitter makeup. And play Barbie dolls."

"Can we, Daddy?" Ashley asked, jumping up.

"As long as you behave like young ladies and not hooligans," he replied.

"What's a hooligan?" Patrick asked.

"I don't know, but my mother always told me not to act like one." He shrugged.

Heather laughed out loud and caught herself before she woke Andrew. "I'm taking this little guy up to his bed."

"Let's go get your stuff," Jessica suggested.

The girls ran toward the bunkhouse.

"That's no fair," Patrick said once he and Mitch were alone.

Mitch ruffled his hair.

"How come you didn't have no boys?" the child asked.

"I would have liked to," he said. "Taylor and Ashley's mother died when they were only two."

"Why don't you get them a new mom and have a boy?"

"That's a good idea," he replied.

"I could teach 'im how to do boy stuff."

Mitch didn't say that they probably wouldn't see each other after the work on the ranch was done and it had been sold. Instead he suggested, "Let's go down to the pond and see if we can catch a frog."

Patrick jumped up with a wide smile. "Okay!"

Mitch had worked on a lot of houses, many of them newer and nicer than this one. But he'd never cared that he wouldn't be the one to enjoy the improvements. This ranch had become more than a job.

And Heather had become more than a client. He watched the boy stride along at his side, the evening breeze ruffling his hair, and knew that when the Johnson family left, there would be an empty spot in his heart.

It was fully dark when Patrick finally consented to allow Mitch to let the frog go back to the pond. "We can catch more," Mitch had promised him.

"You need a bath before bed," his mother said, and accompanied him upstairs.

After washing frog and pond water from his hands, Mitch strolled into the new addition to check the seams of the drywall. Tomorrow the fixtures went in and by the weekend he'd be able to paint.

The accordion doors he'd installed to enclose the washer and dryer still weren't working smoothly, and he spent half an hour adjusting them. "Why, you——" He cussed at the door in frustration.

Straightening, he turned to discover Heather leaning against the doorway, one brow raised in censorship.

"Just the talk I'd expect from a *hooligan*," she admonished.

Heat rose in Mitch's face. "Sorry, I didn't know you were there."

She chuckled. "Give it a rest and come have some lemonade."

He brushed his palms down his jeans and followed

her into the kitchen, where she handed him a glass and led the way to the back porch.

"A swing would be nice, don't you think?" She settled comfortably in the rocker.

"Mmm-hmm." He took a drink. "If you were staying."

She tilted her head. "Right."

The lemonade was tangy and cold and he drank it thirstily. "The girls sleeping?"

"I don't think so, but they're winding down."

"If they keep you awake, come get me and I'll haul 'em back."

"They'll be fine."

Mitch stood to leave and massaged the crick in his neck.

Heather took his glass and set it on the floor beside hers. "Is your neck hurting?"

"It's been stiff ever since shoveling that plaster and spreading the wet cement last week. I think I just strained a muscle."

"Sit on a step and I'll massage it for you."

The offer was too appealing to pass on. He lowered himself to the second step and Heather positioned herself behind him, a knee on each side of his body. She placed both hands low on his neck and smoothed them across his shoulders. Her right hand found a knot and she kneaded it.

A shiver ran through Mitch's body at the profound pleasure. He groaned.

"Right there, isn't it?"

She smelled like lemons and baby shampoo, and her warm thighs bracketed his torso. He straightened and hooked his arms over her knees, allowing their weight to rest on her legs while she did delightful things to his aching neck and shoulders with her small, sturdy hands.

"You're stiff right here," she said, rubbing the spot.

That ain't all, he thought lecherously.

"Are you falling asleep?" The words were breathed right in his ear, and he almost came unglued. Her hands had paused on his shoulders; her breath tickled his ear.

"No." His voice sounded as if he'd eaten gravel for dinner. He raised his hands and covered hers where they lay on his shoulders. His fingertips explored her skin, her knuckles, her short, smooth nails. She turned one hand over, her right one, and it trembled slightly. He traced the contours of her palm and didn't know if he'd ever experienced anything so sensual.

Behind him, though the night was warm and sultry, he sensed her shiver. He used his left hand to capture and hold her right one so she couldn't pull away, and he turned sideways to look up at her.

She didn't try to withdraw, so he released her hand. She used it to touch his hair and trace his ear. It felt too good to be an innocent touch.

Mitch lowered his face and pressed his lips against the skin of her thigh.

A shaky breath escaped her.

He kissed her leg, her knee, darted his tongue out and tasted her. Her flesh quivered under the kiss.

Her left hand, which she'd pressed against his back, knotted his cotton shirt.

Straightening, he raised his head. She lowered hers and their lips met. Not gently this time. Not hesitantly, but hungrily. She bracketed his jaw with her palm and gave herself over to this one.

Her scent enveloped him. Her tart, lemon-tasting kiss devastated him. He could think of nothing but the feel of her lips and the pleasure of her mouth. He wanted to lose himself in her heat and endear himself to her heart. He wanted her. He had a huge gaping place inside him where she belonged.

Disentangling himself briefly, he moved up a step and pulled her into his lap. She came willingly, a warm, enthusiastic participant. He paused for breath and she raised her chin, baring her throat. He nipped it, kissed her skin, nuzzled a path to her ear and closed his teeth gently over her lobe.

Her breath caught and she captured his face and brought his mouth back to hers. "This is crazy," she said, and kissed him again.

Mitch cupped her breast through her cotton top, through her bra, and felt her hardened nipple against his fingers. He wanted to touch her skin, taste her. He wanted to make love to her.

Heather's hand covered his and she pressed herself

against him. "This can't go anywhere," she said against his mouth.

He knew. She'd assured him enough. But he didn't want to think about the lack of a future. He wanted her now. "It doesn't have to mean anything," he said hoarsely.

With her hand on his cheek and his on her breast, she moved away enough to look at him in the darkness. His own words echoed through his head. *It doesn't have to mean anything.* It would mean something to him, something he'd have to live with later—or live without forever.

She meant something to him. How shallow did she think he was to suggest that lovemaking between them could be meaningless?

Apparently he'd said the right thing because she didn't pull away. She brushed the backs of her fingers against his cheek, the beard he'd shaven that morning rasping in the silence.

"I'd better check on the girls," she said softly. "Make sure they're asleep."

And then what?

"I have a baby monitor in the boys's room. I can place it in the hall and bring the receiver with me over to the bunkhouse...if I don't have second thoughts and change my mind."

Mitch's heart pounded. She wanted to come to him. "I hope you don't change your mind."

She disentangled herself from his embrace then, and stood, using his shoulder for support to move up the stairs. He caught her hand and kissed her wrist before she pulled away and entered the house. Don't, don't, *don't* change your mind, he called silently after her. Please, don't change your mind.

He sat there for a few seconds, reliving the heat and the blood-pounding excitement of their kisses. Then, running his fingers through his hair, he stood, glanced behind him into the empty kitchen and headed for the bunkhouse. Stripping off his T-shirt, he shaved in the mottled mirror in the small bathroom, flipped off the lights and went to the screen door to watch for her at the house, which stood dark and proud beneath the moon.

Too many minutes passed.

Mitch worked his boots off and lay on his bunk in the darkness. Stacking his hands beneath his head, he listened to the frogs and the call of an owl through the open door. His erratic heartbeat sounded loud in his ears.

She'd changed her mind.

Disappointment arced through his chest, and desire still pulsed in his blood. Her grip on self-control was for the better, he tried to tell himself. He'd been out of his mind in the heat of passion. He knew this would lead nowhere and he wasn't made to have casual flings. He'd had the foresight to spare a mistake between himself and Trina, and he should have known better than to get carried away with Heather.

But there was no comparison between the women, between his feelings for them.

He should sleep.

A tiny sound caught his attention. An animal perhaps? One of the cats? A board creaked and his heart leaped.

He opened his eyes to her silhouette on the other side of the screen. She'd come.

Eleven

The door squeaked open and closed.

He sat up.

Heather stood framed against the light from the stable that filtered across the porch and through the door. Slender legs in shorts, arms bare, hair falling to her shoulders. He couldn't see her face.

She carried something forward and placed it on the old chest of drawers beside his bunk. "We'll hear if any of them gets up or calls out," she said. "I turned the volume up as high as it'll go."

The receiver made a soft white noise.

"Heather," he said.

She turned toward where he sat. He took her hand and found it trembling.

"If you have any second thoughts about this, I'm not going to push."

"We're both adults," she replied. "We both know the situation."

"What you mean is that you want to be sure I know you're leaving in a few weeks, that this isn't going to lead to anything permanent."

She took a shaky breath. "I haven't done anything for *me* in a very long time." Her voice was low and earnest. "If it's selfish of me to ask this—to want this—I'm sorry. But I can't mislead you."

"You're not selfish. You're one of the most giving people I've ever met."

She sat beside him on the bunk, their hands still clasped. "Sometimes I resent all that giving, so I'm not the saint you imagine. Sometimes I'd like to be on the receiving end."

"I understand." So he spoke what she wanted to hear—what she wanted to believe. "This doesn't have to mean anything except a few hours of pleasure with a person we're attracted to."

She pulled her hand away, almost self-consciously. "I don't do this sort of thing. I've *never* done this before."

"Neither have I."

Her head turned toward him. "Never?"

"There hasn't been anyone since my wife died. I've spent all my energy on the girls and my job."

"I believe you." She hesitated over her next words. "But even though we haven't...had other partners, I don't want to get pregnant, and I haven't used birth control since my divorce."

"I can take care of that."

He got up and strode out to his truck, where he fished in the glove compartment and returned with three square packets. He chuckled as he stuck them under his pillow.

"What's so funny?"

"When I was leaving Minnesota, one of the guys

bought those at a truck stop and told me to enjoy my trip. I laughed, stuck them in the glove compartment and forgot about them.''

He chuckled again.

''What?''

''Nothing. Maybe us discussing this so logically after what happened a little while ago.''

''Have you...lost the urge?''

He smiled. ''I haven't lost the urge since I met you.''

She scooted to the middle of the bunk and tucked her legs up, hugging her knees. ''I'm a little afraid.''

''Of me?''

''No, no. Of what you'll think of me.''

''I'm not going to think any less of you because you want to sleep with me.''

''Not that.'' She lowered her head.

Mitch stroked her silky hair back and tucked it behind her ear. ''What, then?''

''It's silly, I guess.''

He moved close and pulled her against him, kissing the top of her head. ''Tell me.''

''Well, I'm afraid you won't find me...appealing.''

''I already find you appealing.''

''I mean afterward.''

He considered her words. He didn't know much about her husband, or anything about their physical relationship. She'd borne his children, but that didn't necessarily mean she'd had an intimate connection with him. Maybe she was a little shy and awkward about being with a different man. Besides, she'd already assured him there wasn't going to be much "afterward" to worry about.

He closed his arms around her delicate shoulders and hugged her to his chest, burying his face in her hair. "I love the smell of your hair." He lowered his face to the nape of her neck and inhaled. "And your skin."

Heather threaded her arms beneath his to hug him soundly. She loved the solid feel of her breasts crushed against his hard chest, the strength of his arms wrapped around her. She pressed her face to his bare chest, felt the tickle of fine hairs against her nose, inhaled the arousing scent of his flesh that had driven her to this point.

His hands were so gentle on her, his kisses against her neck warm and damp. She was pleased when he turned and lowered them both to their sides on the mattress. He touched her through her clothing, as though discovering her waist, her rib cage and lastly her breasts. The touches were giddily arousing, but unsatisfying because the fabric kept his hands from her skin.

Grateful he wore no shirt, she ran her palms over his chest to satisfy the overwhelming urge to discover his erotic textures. He was steel and satin and heat, and her senses had never been so finely honed to a sensory experience. The skin on the underside of his arm was silky; the hair on his chest, coarse, and she wanted to feel both against her body.

He kissed her finally, a warm, damp seal upon her lips, and she returned the kiss openmouthed. His tongue sought entrance and she met it wholeheartedly. He moved over her, their legs twined, and he pulled her hips against his. Heather could barely stand the sharp edge of desire that had taken control of her senses. Nothing was enough. The kisses weren't enough, the touches weren't enough.

Mitch urged her to sit and tugged upward at the hem of her cotton top. He broke the kiss long enough for her to pull the shirt over her head, then found her lips again. He reached behind her, and after a keen moment of anticipation, unfastened her bra and cast it aside.

The air puckered Heather's nipples, so when he lowered his head he found a tight bud and drew it into his mouth. They'd found a reclining position again, and she grabbed his hair in both hands and heard a sound of pleasure and impatience escape her throat.

"You are perfect," he said, his breath cooling her wet nipple.

"No," she denied.

"Yes." Shifting, he moved to her other breast and favored it with the same devotion.

Heather worried she wasn't giving him near the pleasure he was giving her, but his palm cupping her between her thighs cast her thoughts into oblivion. She pressed against the heel of his hand and gasped.

He reached for the fastening of her shorts and she

helped him, skimming her shorts and panties off in one swoop.

Mitch pushed himself to a standing position, leaving her bare and trembling on his bunk. He had the presence of mind to cross to the door, push it closed and lock it, shutting out the dim light.

Returning, she heard the rasp of his zipper and the rustle of clothing as he removed his jeans.

Her heart pounded erratically. This jolting need was new to her, and only now did she fully recognize her ignorance. She hadn't known she could want a man this way.

His hard thigh met hers, and awakened nerve endings sent the message of pleasure throughout her body.

"I could find you in the dark, just by the way you smell." He knelt on the bed, and his voice came from above her. "It's real, lingering from something you've been doing."

"Peanut butter and jelly turns you on?" she joked nervously. She wasn't accustomed to love talk.

"*You* turn me on." His fingers brushing her abdomen made her skin tingle. He'd become a distinct shape in the darkness now as her eyes adjusted. He stroked her ever so gently with his knuckles. Finally he opened his palm and skimmed it up her ribs to the outside of her breast, and she breathed a sigh of relief that he was touching her again at last.

Lifting her upper body from the mattress, she reached for his shoulders and pulled him down to her.

His fuzzy chest came in contact with her sensitive breasts; his arousal pressed hot and provocative against her hip. She barely stifled a moan. His leisurely seduction was going to drive her mad.

Guiding his chin, she initiated an abandoned kiss. He touched her then, finding her slick and swollen in readiness. His caress was deliberate, yet unhurried, and once she realized he had no intention of entering her quickly and bringing their coupling to a rushed end, she relaxed and accepted the intense pleasure.

She melted against him, allowing the sensations to build and build. His patience and deliberation humbled her, thrilled her.

Heather's body stiffened and her climax swept over her in a keen wave. A little disappointed and a lot embarrassed at her swift release, she opened her eyes to Mitch's dark outline above her. He kissed her chin, her throat, tasted her and trailed a damp path to her breast. When he pulled her nipple between his teeth, a corresponding pulsing ache throbbed to new life.

He reached beneath the pillow, then deftly sheathed himself and returned to enter her. Heather gripped his upper arms and shuddered at the pleasurable sensation.

He began a slow, tantalizing rhythm that rocked her senses and renewed her feverish desire. Heather almost cried at the fierce edge of gratification.

He whispered against her neck, hot unsettling words and praises in a heart-stirring voice. She quivered at the passion in his lovemaking, at the force of her physical and emotional reaction.

When he grasped her hips and dropped his forehead into the crook of her neck and spent himself, Heather spun over the edge with a gasp.

The wild rhythm of his heart against her breast slowed and the air cooled their damp skin. Mitch slid his weight to her side and cradled her. She'd heard and read a lot of hype about passionate lovemaking, and she'd always believed two things: that the stories were exaggerated, and that her experiences were lacking. Now she knew only one was true.

When she went home and got back to her normal life, she would always know that she'd finally experienced something incredible with the most unselfish and warmhearted man she'd ever known. Surely he had some negative qualities that would lessen her opinion of him, but he hadn't yet revealed them. And the good part of a brief fling such as this was that there wouldn't be a chance for her to see them—and even if she did, she could ignore them until she left, never have to deal with him again.

Her calculated thinking almost shamed her, but she buried the guilt in favor of doing something for herself for a change. She hadn't given him false hope. Not that he'd even want anything more, she scoffed at herself. She wasn't exactly a hot prize, and he might even lose interest before their time together was over.

"That was incredible," he said against her temple.

"I had no idea," she replied on a sigh.

He had sensed Heather's uncertainty with each progressive phase of their lovemaking, uncertainty overcome by desire, and almost...well, wonder or surprise.

Mitch enjoyed her soft damp skin against his, her hair under his chin, and the beat of her heart beneath his arm. She was so erotically responsive and fervent, his body remained half aroused. He wasn't sorry. Even though this woman was now a part of his very heart, he wasn't sorry.

He wouldn't try to change her mind. Pressure was no foundation for a relationship. It hurt him to the core that she didn't have the same feelings he did, but he was a big boy. He'd walked into this with his eyes wide open.

Mitch disentangled his limbs from Heather's, made a trip to the bathroom, left the light on and the door ajar, and returned to find her beneath the sheet. "Cold?"

"A little."

Her self-consciousness was endearing. He slid alongside her and followed the curves of her body through the fabric. She avoided his eyes. "Are you sorry?"

That brought her gaze to his. "No."

"Good." He tilted up her chin and kissed her.

"Are you?"

Oh, yes. Sorry that he couldn't say more. Sorry that all they'd ever share would be stolen moments in the night. Sorry she didn't need or want more. Somehow she'd kindled a fire in him that wouldn't be squelched by a few nights of abandon. "No."

"Good." She traced his jaw. "Did you shave just for me?"

He nodded.

"I noticed."

She caressed her fingertips across his smooth chin, lowered her thumb to the hollow at his throat, then raised her index finger to his lower lip.

Her arousing touches started his blood pounding. He took the tip of her finger into his mouth, and she inhaled sharply. She withdrew it and kissed him.

"It's only fair to warn you that you're starting something," he said with a growl. He pressed himself against her through the barrier of the sheet.

"That's not a warning." She gave him a flirtatious smile. "That's an invitation."

Twelve

The following morning, Heather climbed out of her bed and into the shower, pleasurably sore and completely enamored.

Mitch spoke about sex in a frank, down-to-earth way, and he made love in the same manner, unsparingly, energetically.

As the water sluiced down her newly awakened body, she savored every remembered moment up until he'd sent her back to the house, telling her he wouldn't risk another session until he'd gone into town and visited the pharmacy.

Dressing, she discovered herself smiling irrepressibly and paused in front of the mahogany-framed mirror, the sight so foreign that she pulled herself up short. She couldn't remember ever being happy in this house. There had never been one cheerful association until now.

She leaned forward and touched her lips, her neck, her collarbone. She'd lived almost thirty years without the affection of anyone except the children she'd given birth to, and Mitch's attentions would sidetrack her if she wasn't careful. Enjoy it, she told herself, but remember where you came from and where you're going. Don't get caught up and forget.

Youthful voices alerted her that the kids were awake. She greeted them, then helped the boys dress. "Want help with your hair?" she asked Jess.

Her daughter handed her the brush and an elastic band.

"That's pretty," Taylor said a few minutes later as Heather neared the end of the French braid.

Heather watched Taylor's revealing expression in the mirror. "Would you like me to fix your hair this way?" she asked the girl.

The child glanced down for a moment, then looked up and nodded shyly.

"Will you do mine, too, Heather?" Ashley asked, not the least inhibited with her request.

It was almost a half hour later when Heather helped Andrew descend the stairs.

"I'm hungry for pannycakes, Mama." Patrick opened the back door, allowing the fresh morning air and sunshine to permeate the kitchen.

"Pancakes it is," she said, gathering the ingredients.

"Wanna help set the table?" Jess asked the twins. She showed them how to arrange the plates and silverware.

"Shall we see if Mitch wants to eat with us, Mama?" Jess asked, her usual thoughtful self. "They only have cereal at the bunkhouse."

Heather hefted a heavy griddle onto the stove and

turned on the burner. "Might as well. Andrew, you stay here with me."

The girls and Patrick tore out the back door, and returned a few minutes later. "He was still sleepin'," Patrick informed her. "We woked him."

"He'll be here in a little bit," Jess said.

Heather imagined him sleeping in after his exhausting night and being awakened by this pack of rowdy hooligans. She grinned.

The kids were seated and on their second batch of pancakes when his boots hit the porch floor and the door creaked open. Heather's heart tripped irrationally.

Dressed in worn, clean jeans, a form-fitting T-shirt, his hair damp from a shower, he was the best thing Heather had ever laid eyes on. He greeted the kids with a smile, then his gaze shifted to hers. "Morning."

"Morning," she managed to say around the erratic beat of her heart in her throat. She hadn't stopped thinking about last night; even her dreams had been sultry and vivid. Seeing him made her throat tight and her chest burn. What was wrong with her?

Ashley hugged him and Mitch picked her up for a squeeze. She wrapped her legs around his waist and her arms around his neck. "Did you get lonesome last night, Daddy?"

"Only a little. Your hair is beautiful! Yours, too, Taylor. And Jessica. Have you girls been to the beauty shop already this morning?"

"No, silly," Ashley said. "Heather did our hair."

"Your hidden talents never cease to amaze me," he drawled over Ashley's shoulder. "Pancakes, too."

Heather's face grew hot. "Sit down and eat before they get cold."

He lowered Ashley and took a seat. After the first taste, he rolled his eyes. "Hot and sweet, just the way I like them."

His playful teasing was unexpected, but she enjoyed the familiarity of his underlying messages.

"Maybe you'll feel like making them again tomorrow morning."

"Maybe I will," she replied. They flirted and grinned and bantered like…lovers.

Heather rolled the word around in her head. Lovers.

Perhaps that was a trifle too strong for what they really meant to each other.

What *did* they mean to each other?

She caught herself and arrested the thoughts that had buoyed her all morning. A summer fling was not a true test for the reality of a permanent relationship. Losing her head over this sexy man did not justify the loss of herself and her freedom. She wasn't willing to lock herself into the bondage of marriage again, so keeping things in perspective had to be her goal.

But as he finished his breakfast and sauntered out the door, casting a sexy smile just for her over his shoulder, she knew keeping him in perspective would be no easy task.

* * *

Her seeming aversion to this ranch wasn't consistent with the enjoyment she took in being here, Mitch thought the next day, watching Heather lead their five children home from an excursion in the foothills. She and Jessica carried buckets, which from this distance appeared to be filled with berries.

From his position on the roof, he watched their approach with amusement. The closer they got, the clearer he could see the stains on all their hands and faces. The older children broke into a run and headed for the swings. Heather picked up Andrew, spotted Mitch and waved.

He returned the greeting, noting her lips were as red as Andrew's chin. He'd like to taste her right now.

Glancing over at Ronnie, he wielded his hammer and returned to his work. There was an endearing streak of defiance underlying Heather's precise and orderly character, and he would love to know what made her tick. Her pleasure in caring for the kids and preparing them meals was apparent in every task she performed. She didn't act like a city woman being put out by this turn of events.

Words were the only expression of her desire to get away from the ranch and go back to California. But words were strong.

That evening, he had put the girls to bed and was on the porch of the bunkhouse, going over the blueprints by lantern light, when Heather called from her back porch. "Phone for you!"

He crossed the distance to the house and entered

the kitchen. She handed him a cup of coffee, pointed with a blue paint-stained finger to the receiver lying on the counter, then disappeared into the newly remodeled room beyond.

He wiped a smudge of wet paint from the phone with a napkin. "Hello?"

"Mitch, how is the project going?" His grandfather's voice greeted him.

"Just great."

"Good. Good. I'm planning something for Saturday. A barbecue. I thought it would be good to get you brothers together. Will you be here?"

"What time?"

"Two."

"We'll be there."

They exchanged a few pleasantries and Mitch hung up. He found Heather in the combination laundry and bath. She had taped off the lower half of the walls and was painting a small section blue with a roller. As soon as she got the section painted, she set the roller aside and, using both hands, crimped a rag and manipulated it over the area, taking paint off in a eye-pleasing pattern.

"What are you doing?"

"Rag rolling. I saw it on the home and garden channel. It's not as easy as it looks. If you don't roll over it fast enough, the paint dries. You really need extra hands."

"How about if I roll the paint and you do the 'frou-frou thing'?"

She looked at him over her shoulder. "The 'frou-frou thing'?"

He picked up the roller. "Go."

They worked that way for about forty-five minutes, until Heather stopped and rolled her shoulders and neck. "This takes arm strength."

Mitch snorted. "Let me try."

"This is the section the washer will cover. I guess you can practice."

He raised a brow as though insulted, and bent to the task.

She laughed at his first attempts, but once he got the hang of it, the walls were finished in no time.

"You can add interior decorator to your résumé now," she teased.

"I don't think so." He washed the roller and pan in the deep metal sink he had installed. "How come you're doing this, anyway, if you're just putting the place up for sale?"

She scrubbed paint from under her fingernails and shrugged. "I wanted the room to look finished. I ordered some wallpaper border that has quilts hanging on a clothesline."

"I'm sure the new owners will appreciate the touch." He found his cup on a paint-speckled ladder, sipped and grimaced.

"I can make some fresh," she said.

"No, don't bother."

They entered the kitchen, and Mitch placed his cup in the sink. He turned and noted the set of monitor units resting atop the checkered cloth on the oak table. He cast a suggestive glance at Heather, and she blushed.

"I'd better go check on the girls." He turned away.

"Coming back?"

He turned and found her calmly straightening a stack of papers beneath the phone, as though the question hadn't been loaded. "Want me to?"

She nodded. "You could take the baby unit and leave it beside them."

"This one?" At her nod, he picked it up and left.

When he returned, she was sitting on the porch. "You shaved."

"How'd you know?"

"I heard you." She lifted the white plastic monitor unit and grinned. Setting it on the porch floor, she stood and moved against him, reaching to caress his smooth jaw. "Nice."

He kissed her gently.

"You made a trip to town." She smoothed a finger over his chin.

He nodded, knowing what she was getting at. "We're okay."

He kissed her again.

The surge of sensuality he created with a simple kiss surprised her anew. She wondered if she was exciting enough for him, adventuresome enough. She knew little of flirtation or seduction, and he seemed a man deserving of both.

He tugged her flush against him and caressed her

back, running a thumb down her spine, lowering his
hands to her bottom and cupping her through her
shorts. "Where do you want to go?"

She'd thought about it the whole time he'd been
checking on the girls and shaving. "My room."

He turned her in his loose embrace and guided her
forward. "Lead the way."

Thirteen

Clasping his hand, she led him through the house, to the stairs, and up. He followed her quietly along the hallway and into the room she used. It had been her mother's room, and she'd chosen it because it held no memories. Undoubtedly it would after tonight.

Mitch closed the door. "Is there a lock?"

"There's a skeleton key in the lock."

He found and turned it. "Can we have a light?"

She hesitated.

"I didn't get to see you the other night. If all we're going to have are these short times together, I'd like to have more to remember than the feel of you in the dark."

Her face warmed at his words. Always frank, this man. Always honest. She made her way to the low oak dressing table and turned the switch on the painted glass boudoir lamp, catching her image in the mirror.

Mitch stepped up behind her and glanced over the few bottles and jars on the tabletop. His gaze raised to hers in the glass.

He lifted the hem of her cotton shirt, revealing the

waistband of her shorts and her skin above. He tugged higher. "Raise your arms."

Heather obeyed and helped him removed her top. His fingers went to work on the clasp of her bra and had it loose in seconds.

Her instinct was to clutch it to her breasts, but his breath touched her shoulder and her hands fell to her sides. The garment slid down her arms to the floor. Any confidence she'd gained up to this point wavered. Her flaws were glaringly apparent in the lamplight. Three pregnancies had done a number on her body. But he studied her reflection, his eyes full of appreciation. She wasn't young or girlishly firm, but whatever he saw must have pleased him.

Smiling, he kissed her shoulder.

"You're embarrassing me," she said.

He spanned her waist, caressed her ribs, smoothed his rough palms up her arms, down her back and under her arms to cup her breasts. "You don't have anything to be embarrassed about."

Sighing, Heather let her head fall back against him. "I don't know how to do this."

She raised a hand to his jaw, and when he lowered his face, she tipped hers to meet his tender kiss.

He bent to her neck and nipped her there, bit her flesh, then covered the tingling spot with his warm damp lips. She wanted to turn and close herself against him, but he held her firmly against his chest. "What don't you know how to do?"

She shook the thoughts away. "The least you could do is take your shirt off."

"Impatient?" he asked, and she liked his torturous teasing. His hands went to her waistband where he unbuttoned and unzipped her shorts. Flattening his palm, he stroked her abdomen, then beneath the elastic of her panties. He withdrew and slid her remaining clothing down her hips to the floor.

Heather kicked the soft pile aside.

His heated gaze absorbed her flesh in the mirror, adoring her, kindling her. He massaged her hips, stroked the globes of her bottom and pulled her back hard against him.

The denim of his jeans was a foreign texture, a nuisance and an erotic incitement to her bare flesh.

"Sit and let me brush your hair."

He turned her inside out and she couldn't stop herself from following his gentle request. He pulled out the bench and she stepped around it to sit on the cool brocade padding.

Mitch picked up a hairbrush and proceeded to draw it through her hair, from the front to the back, the roots to the ends. He was quite good at it, and she remembered he had two daughters to tend to each day. This was no morning duty, however; this was an arousing stage of foreplay he carried to its fullest.

Tears smarted behind her eyelids, and Heather blinked them away and closed her lids. No one had ever been so tender with her. She'd never known beauty or gentleness such as this man bestowed.

She'd believed she'd known what sex was about, but she hadn't possessed a clue until now. With Craig it had been a joining of bodies, but with Mitch it was mating of spirits. A touching of souls and hearts that equally amazed and frightened her.

"Did I hurt you?" The brushing stopped and he spoke against her ear, his voice ragged with repentance. "I'm sorry."

"No." She opened her eyes. He was looking at her, not in the mirror, not at her nakedness, but at *her*, with concern and genuine regret. She turned her head and met his eyes. "You didn't hurt me. Far from it. I'm sorry...it's just all so different."

"But the tears..." With an unsteady thumb, he brushed away moisture she hadn't realized had made its way to her cheek.

"Tears of desire," she said softly, unwilling to admit even to herself how deeply he touched her. "How long will you make me wait?"

He tossed the brush onto the tabletop and reached for her. She stood and he gathered her close. Taking her hand, he led her to the bed. As Heather pulled back the comforter, Mitch removed his clothing and met her in the middle of the soft mattress. He wasn't the least bit inhibited about his desire for her, nor did he hold back in showing her what he liked when she reached to touch him.

Heather's experience grew by leaps and bounds at his unrestrained tutoring. She'd always thought sex was more enjoyable for men, but he blew that theory out of the water. At last he stretched out over her and entered her. Heather grasped the sheets while he relentlessly rocked her up against the mahogany headboard and into damp, rumpled ecstasy.

She enjoyed the weight of him as he caught his breath and his heart rate gradually returned to normal. Trailing her fingers over his back, she marveled at how right they were together, how nothing else mattered at that moment, but the fulfillment she felt in his arms.

Moving to her side, he pulled her into his embrace and held her. The entire universe revolved inside that room at that moment.

"You're so full of wonderful surprises," she said sleepily.

"What's so surprising?" he asked.

"You. Me. Us. This."

"Think you could explain in more than one-word sentences?"

She smiled against his warm skin. "No."

They lay that way, with him lazily rubbing his thumb up and down her spine. After a time, Mitch roused and looked into her eyes. "I'd better go check on the girls."

She chuckled against his chest.

"You think I'm nuts."

"Not at all." He moved to a sitting position and she propped her head on her hand. "I understand completely. Go ahead. We'd have heard something if they'd made a sound, but you should be assured."

"Okay." He leaned forward and gave her a brief kiss. "I'll be right back. I just need to double check."

"Go."

He stood, located his jeans, and quickly pulled them on. With a sheepish expression, he leaned over and gave her a sweet kiss before unlocking the door and disappearing into the dark hall.

Heather pulled the sheet up and rested her head on the pillow. Beneath the crisp cotton her skin was still alive and hypersensitive. She'd abandoned her inhibitions and made glorious, intoxicating love with the man. He approached the act as he did everything else, with consideration and energy and an obvious amount of experience under his belt.

The sound of the bunkhouse door echoed from the monitor. He was barefoot, but she could hear the creak of floorboards and then a rustle.

"Miss me?"

The whisper echoed from the monitor, a trifle distorted, but plainly Mitch's voice. She smiled.

She heard him use the bathroom and once again the sound of the door. A minute later he appeared in the hallway.

"Yes," she replied to his earlier whispered question.

He approached the bed and stretched out full-length beside her. "They were sound asleep."

She nodded.

He faced her and feathered touches along her arm. Once again, Heather snuggled into comfortable closeness, cherishing each minute so unique and different from her experience.

"I get the impression that it wasn't like this with your husband," he said, as though he'd been reading her mind. Maybe he didn't have to read her mind. Maybe her ignorance was embarrassingly obvious.

The comment caught her off guard. "Ex-husband." She really didn't want to expound. There was nothing to say, really. Nothing.

"Ex-husband," he agreed. "So what was it like?"

She flattened a palm over his heart. "Not like this."

"No?"

"No." Mitch was so open and honest, and she hated the fear she experienced at the thought of opening up to him. She mentally chastised herself. She had an incredible man in her bed, a man willing to talk and listen, besides share what they'd just shared.

He was interested, genuinely interested, and the dangerous knowledge was intoxicating. She was drunk on Mitch.

She rolled onto her back, threw an arm above her head, and studied the ceiling with a sigh. "I thought I'd experienced it. I thought because I'd had sex with the man once or twice a week for nearly ten years that I knew what it was about. I was wrong."

"This is different?"

He was curious, not fishing for compliments. She knew him well enough to know that. So for the first time she shared something personal—besides her body—with him. "What you and I share isn't about control. It's not about duty."

He didn't say anything, and she turned to read confusion in his eyes.

"There's a—a freedom I've never known."

"Freedom from what?"

She couldn't even begin to tell him. "Bondage."

"You mean, marriage."

"From worrying that I'll do something wrong. From never just being myself for fear it's not good enough. From showing my pay stub as proof that I'm an equal partner."

He dragged the sheet to her waist and traced a lazy circle around her nipple with his fingertip. "What about the good times? What about in the beginning?"

"In the beginning I was simply grateful to get away from here."

"What did you want to get away from?"

She'd said too much already. Even in privacy, she didn't examine the loneliness and neglect of her childhood; she wasn't about to open a door to a subject she had closed off. "What about you?" she asked, changing the direction. "You and your wife."

He flattened his palm against her chest as though it took all his concentration to remember. "It was good."

"Real good?" She couldn't imagine anything better than how it had been between the two of them. And for some reason it bothered her to think of this man with the woman he'd loved.

"We were in love," he stated, and it probably did explain a lot. She wouldn't know. She had started out thinking she loved Craig. She had tried.

"You were happy?"

"Yes."

"I'm sorry. Sorry you lost her, I mean."

"You know what's hard?" he asked.

"Tell me."

"When people avoid talking about Jamie, or saying her name. Like she never happened. Like they can't say it around me or I'll go to pieces or something." He told her how his life had gone from near perfect to tragic in the space of a year. How he stayed strong for Jamie and the girls, but how he'd wanted to burst apart and rage at the unfairness.

"Some days I didn't think I could go on," he said, his lips against her skin. "But I did. And four years have passed."

"And now?"

He inhaled. "Now I've faced the fact that I have gone on, and that I will go on. Now I can remember the good things, rather than the pain and the loss that was all there was at first. She would want me to be happy."

Happy with a woman who welcomed him into her bed, but not into her heart? He'd had the real thing once. Heather envied him for it. She envied his dead wife. "Think she'd approve of a fling with a divorcée?"

He grew still beside her. Her heart raced in the

strained silence. She'd wounded him in her dogmatic determination to make sure he didn't romanticize this thing into anything more than it was.

"You make it sound cheap," he said at last.

"I didn't mean it like that. I'm sorry."

He sat up then, facing away from her on the edge of the bed. "I'll get over it."

She rested a hand on his shoulder. "Mitch, I'm sorry."

"Okay." He turned and his gaze touched her soul. "I'd better go get some sleep. Good night."

Heather's mind crowded with desperate ravings. He didn't deserve to be hurt. She didn't want him to leave. She needed him to hold her until this frantic need passed, until she could absorb the hurtful words back inside her where they belonged.

But there was no choice. She'd already laid out the dictates of their relationship. They'd gone too far tonight, shared too much, been too intimate. She wanted him. She was afraid of him.

She was afraid of herself.

Fourteen

The air between them was tense the following day, and Heather knew it was her fault. She'd drawn a line, more clearly and forcefully than before. Within the frame of Mitch's love and respect for his wife, she'd made what the two of them had shared seem tawdry. Doing so had hurt him. Doing so had hurt her. But she wouldn't have taken it back.

When she called him for lunch, he sat on the back porch with the girls, and she left them to their time alone.

That night he left and took the girls to Billings for pizza, and Heather didn't see them when they returned.

On Friday afternoon Heather received a call from her boss. Their important project couldn't wait any longer. After six weeks of delay, they were going to move forward without her. They'd hired a consultant to finish the work.

She moved through the afternoon in a fog of confusion. For so long her work had defined her; now being unneeded changed how she saw herself. She'd given years to the firm, but it went on operating without her. Those years seemed insignificant. Her work seemed insignificant.

That, combined with the strain between her and Mitch, caused her attitude and confidence to waver.

She took all the kids except Jessica for a walk in the foothills and returned to find her daughter sitting on the porch steps.

"We got a call," Jess told her.

Immediately Heather thought of her boss in San Francisco.

"It was Mitch's grampa. He wants you to call him. I wrote the number down."

"Thanks, honey."

Heather dialed the number Jess had taken and waited while the woman who answered the phone went to get Garrett.

"Heather," he said. "Thanks for getting back to me. We haven't met yet. I'm Mitch's grandfather, Garrett Kincaid."

"I'm glad to hear from you," she said kindly.

"I'm having a little get-together at my ranch tomorrow and I'm hoping this isn't too late of a notice to invite you to come."

"Well, I—"

"Do you already have plans?"

"No, but—"

"Well, then, there's no reason why you can't join us for the afternoon."

"I have the children," she said.

"There'll be other kids here. I'm planning something special for them, in fact. Be here at two."

"Well, all right. Thank you."

"Great. See you then."

She hung up the phone and puzzled over the odd invitation, wondering if Mitch had put him up to it. But why would he if he was avoiding her, which seemed to be the case the past two days.

"Come in for supper?" she asked Mitch after his workers had gone for the day. He was making a pile of old boards.

"I need to shower," was his reply.

"We'll wait for you."

He straightened and met her eyes finally. "All right."

After placing his power tools in his lockbox, he headed for the bunkhouse.

Heather called the children to wash and help her set the table. Patrick climbed up and settled on a chair. "I'm gonna sit by Mitch."

"That's my place," Taylor objected.

"I'm here first."

"He's my dad."

Heather saw the hurt in Patrick's eyes the moment the words left Taylor's lips.

"I got a dad," Patrick said defensively.

"Where is he?" Ashley's eyebrows rose inquisitively. "Is he in heaven like our mommy?"

"He's in Los Angeles," Jessica replied matter-of-factly. "He doesn't live with us."

"Why not?"

"'Cause him and my mom got a divorce," Jessica said.

Ashley accepted that explanation. "Oh."

Heather placed dishes of vegetables on the table. "Taylor, would you like to sit by me, so Patrick can have a turn beside your dad?"

"I wanna sit by you," Ashley piped up immediately.

"That's nice, honey. Patrick, you move to the chair on the other side of Mitch's, okay?"

"Okay."

The seating was finally arranged by the time Mitch arrived, scrubbed and wet-haired. Heather passed food, served for the kids, and got warm bread from the oven.

"Garrett invited us to his ranch tomorrow." She stood just behind him and spoke softly so only he could hear.

"For the barbecue? That's nice."

"Would you rather we didn't go?" The mealtime chatter covered her words.

He turned to glance at her. "Why would I not want you to go?"

Indeed. Why not? He was getting pretty good at ignoring her. "I just wondered."

She took her seat at the other end of the table.

"I don't want to eat this," Taylor said, poking her slice of roast with her fork.

Mitch deftly reached over to spear it from her plate,

sliced the tender meat and ate it without a word of discussion on the subject. The child sat forward and ate her potatoes, gravy, and vegetables with apparent enjoyment.

Mitch cracked a smile and glanced at Heather.

They shared a moment of silent gratitude and relief over the food problem that had been resolved since they'd met.

"Wanna catch some frogs after supper, Mitch?" Patrick asked.

"You know, sport, I was thinking I was going to take the girls and go visit my brother, Cade. Thanks for asking me, though. We'll do it another day. All right?"

Patrick nodded, and Heather sensed his disappointment. Mitch must have, too. He leaned over and gave Heather's son a hug. "I promise."

Patrick grinned then.

It was her he was avoiding, not Patrick, Heather realized with a measure of guilt. He'd always seemed to have time for the kids, hers as well as his own, whether it was to tie a shoe or to read a bedtime story or to catch frogs.

Getting involved on a physical level had impaired their relationship, and now everyone had to suffer. She'd known it would happen, but she'd been greedy. Selfish. Now they all had to pay.

Without helping clear the table, Mitch excused them and ushered the girls to the bunkhouse. Heather was finishing the dishes when she heard his truck start and pull away.

She busied herself with going through file cabinets in her father's study that evening. She'd become lax and forgotten her purpose here. There was still a lot to be done before she could sell the ranch and empty the house.

She'd been procrastinating.

Sitting at her father's desk, sorting papers and packing a box, she faced the truth.

Being forced to stay and renovate the house had been the excuse she needed, and she'd hidden behind it for weeks now. Finding her employer could get along just fine without her was not as devastating as it should have been—if she'd truly derived all her self-worth from her work.

Perhaps that approval wasn't all that important anymore. Perhaps she'd finally slowed down enough to see what it was she really needed—and wanted. And perhaps that reality was frightening her.

She'd had time to get to know her children better and to develop a stronger relationship with each of them. She'd raised some pretty fine kids, and that was an incomparable accomplishment.

She'd enjoyed every day here with them.

She'd begun to think that proving her worth wasn't impressing anybody anymore. But she was so good at fooling herself that she'd fooled everyone else, including Mitch.

Heather rubbed her fingers across the scarred desktop, studied the black-and-white photograph of her mother, a woman she didn't remember, and toyed with a brass letter opener.

She didn't see much of herself in the woman's face. The woman whose death had so destroyed her father that he'd shut out the world. Heather had forgiven him, years ago in counseling. But that hadn't erased the sadness or the nagging thoughts of how things might have been different.

She'd never proved her worth to her father. Pete Bolton had never taken note of her or her accomplishments, small or large. Craig Johnson had only seen the value in her earning power, not in her as a person.

She was okay, she told herself. Heather Bolton had been an okay child, someone to be proud of. Heather Johnson was a good mother and a worthwhile person. She had a lot of good qualities, and could probably list them if a person asked her to.

She still had a lot of healing and growing to do.

But she would do it.

"What are we doing today, Mom?" Jess asked. They'd cleared away breakfast, and Heather was standing at the door, sipping a cup of tea.

She turned to her daughter, who sat at the table, a book open in front of her, and a realization came to her: she hadn't planned the morning. She chuckled to herself. "We don't have to be at Mitch's grandfather's until two. What do you want to do until we have to get ready?"

Jessica's eyebrows rose. "Really? Cool! I was just looking at this book of fun things for kids to do."

Heather came to peer over her shoulder. "What is that, clay?"

Jessica ran her finger down the columns of instructions until she came to the ingredient list. "It's just cornstarch and stuff. You make it up into modeling clay and shape it and bake it. See?"

Heather read over the list of simple ingredients. "We can try that. The boys will love it."

"All right! This is gonna be fun!"

"And there's nothing in it that will hurt Andrew if he eats it," she said with a smile.

"Don't you mean 'when' he eats it?" Jess asked.

They laughed and Heather called the boys.

Andrew did eat some of the pasty clay, but he spit it out and asked for a drink.

"Must not be as tasty as crayons," Heather said to Jessica, and they shared another laugh, one of many that morning. Before she knew it, she glanced at the clock and realized she hadn't thought about their lunch yet.

The freedom of allowing the day to come to them, without planning and plotting, was a new and liberating experience, one she'd fallen into quite easily—thanks to Mitch's help.

He talked as though she'd been the one to make all the positive changes—helping with the twins and their eating dilemma. But he'd brought about some changes in her, as well, by making her look at the benefits of being flexible.

"Look at my horse, Mama," Patrick said. "Can we bake 'im now?"

Footsteps hit the back porch and the kitchen door flew open, startling all of them. Taylor stood inside the doorway, her blue eyes wide with her unshed tears.

"Heather! Heather! Ashley's cryin' and she won't stop!"

They hadn't seen the girls that morning, as Mitch hadn't joined the crew who had shown up to scrape and paint the west side of the house. It was Saturday, and she'd figured he was spending some time with his daughters.

"Jess, watch the boys," Heather said calmly, and let Taylor take her hand and lead her toward the bunkhouse. The child urged her into a run. "What's wrong, honey? Is your sister hurt?"

"You gotta come, is all. You gotta help or she won't never stop cryin'."

Ashley's cries were audible before they reached the porch and Heather experienced a moment of panic. What on *earth* had happened?

Fifteen

Taylor pulled Heather up the steps and yanked open the screen door.

Heather held back, torn between not wanting to intrude on a family crisis and wanting to help if she could. She called out, "Mitch? Ashley?"

Mitch stood at the foot of a bunk where Ashley lay facedown on her pillow, great wailing sobs shaking her small body.

"Ashley Nicole Fielding, you stop that racket right this minute," Mitch said forcefully. "Now you've got your hair a wilder mess than ever."

"I told ya," Taylor said, staring imploringly up at Heather.

Heather took a few steps closer. "Is there anything I can do?"

"Heather!" Ashley practically flung herself into Heather's arms. "It gots to be a fresh braid, and he said it was f-fine the way h-he did it. But it wasn't! I told 'im y-you could do it right."

"I redid it three times," Mitch said helplessly. "She kept saying she wanted a fresh braid, and I can't get it any fresher than that."

One side of Ashley's blond hair stuck out as a result of her conniption fit on the bed, but the back was fashioned into a passable braided tail. "It looks pretty good to me," Heather told the near-hysterical girl. She wrapped an arm around her and patted her back. "It's not bad at all, sweetie."

"But it's not a *fresh* braid, Heather. I want it to be special to go to the party at my grandpa's."

"A fresh— Oh my goodness! You mean a *French* braid!"

Ashley nodded vigorously. "Tell 'im you can do it right."

Heather turned and studied Mitch's confused face with sympathy. "She wants a French braid. Like I fixed their hair the other morning."

"I don't know how to do that."

"Here." She went into the bathroom, returned with a wet washcloth, and bathed Ashley's rosy tear-stained face. "A smile is as important as pretty hair," she told her, and gave her another hug. "Let's see that pretty smile."

Ashley gave her a weak but valiant smile.

"That's my girl. Now sit on the stool over here."

The child climbed onto the wooden stool and Taylor ran to bring Heather a comb and brush. "Will you do mine, too? Please?" Heather nodded, removed the hair band from the current braid and set to work, feeling Mitch's penetrating gaze the entire time.

Finished at last, she admired the results and the girls thanked her.

Feeling foolish, Mitch walked her to the door. "It's

not that often that we have a hair emergency. I suppose it'll happen more and more the older they get.''

"I can teach you how."

Capable, efficient Heather. He shrugged noncommittally. It was better that he kept his distance, though he'd realized it a little late. He shouldn't have allowed his better judgment to be impaired by his raging physical hunger for her. She'd warned him a dozen times. He'd ignored the warnings, believing he could handle his head and his feelings and his heart.

But no.

He knew his own character. He'd rationalized his inability for casual flings when Trina had come on to him. He'd known then that he couldn't involve his body without his head. He'd known the same where Heather was concerned, too, but he hadn't detoured. Some irrationally foggy part of his brain had imagined that she'd fall for him. That she'd be unable to live without him.

What a jerk.

If there was a jerk hall of fame, he'd be this year's inductee. "I'll see you later," he said.

With a sideways glance, she moved out onto the porch and down the stairs.

"Heather?"

She paused and turned.

"Thank you."

She nodded and went on. "You're welcome."

Mitch loaded the girls into his truck, even though they had plenty of time before the barbecue started.

They would arrive early and he could help with preparations. If he stayed here much longer, it would be logical to ride together, and he didn't want to put either of them in the position of being seen together and having anyone make assumptions.

Mitch had been thinking more and more about a permanent move to Whitehorn. It was perfectly logical and natural. His step-siblings were scattered across the states and his mother and stepfather were retired and wanted to travel now. Garrett, Mitch's newfound brothers and land of his own were a draw he couldn't deny.

But Heather had no intention of staying in Whitehorn. She couldn't wait to get back to California. These feelings for her had nowhere to grow. Planting them and nurturing them could only mean pain. He knew the heartbreak of loss firsthand, and he couldn't bear it again.

Garrett had hired a rental company to set up tables and chairs in the shade beside the house. Directed by Leanne Redstone, several efficient-looking men and woman were making drinks and setting out stacks of plates. A hog was roasting on an open spit.

"That's gross!" Taylor made a face that plainly showed her disgust. "Why did they do that to that pig?"

"That's what pigs are for," he explained. "We eat pork all the time, but it's made into bacon and chops and roasts and ham and you just don't see the whole thing."

"Ham is not so a pig."

"What is it, then?"

"It's meat."

He'd be wise to shut up or he'd have another food trauma on his hands. "You don't have to eat it. You don't even have to look at it."

"I can't stop looking at it. It's terrible!"

"It is terrible, Daddy," Ashley agreed.

"It is pretty gross," he admitted after another assessing glance. "I don't think I'll eat any, either."

"Can't they cover him up?"

"I'll ask Grandpa," Mitch replied. He distracted them by setting up the croquet game and practicing shots.

Mitch noticed a dark blue, newer-model car winding up the drive toward the house. He left the girls for a moment and walked toward the slowing vehicle. A door opened and a long-limbed, voluptuous blonde climbed out.

The front door opened and Collin stepped out of the house at the same time Mitch reached the woman.

"Can I help you? Are you here for the barbecue?" Mitch asked, though her dark green suit wasn't attire for a backyard get-together.

"I don't think I'd get a warm reception at a Kincaid gathering," she replied with a wry smile. "I've come to deliver papers to Garrett." The folder she held verified her business. She stretched a hand toward Mitch. "Hope Baxter."

Mitch introduced himself and shook her hand.

Collin took her hand next, and it seemed to Mitch that the contact was drawn out a little too long. His half brother studied the young woman with interest. "Nice to meet you. I'm Collin Kincaid."

Her soft blue-gray eyes returned the perusal. Finally she pulled her hand away.

"Hope is Jordan's daughter," Collin said to Mitch. "His attorney, actually."

The connection clicked in Mitch's mind. This woman was handling the legal details to keep them from inheriting the ranch. Naturally Garrett wouldn't have invited her to the party. But how could Mitch have known?

"That's right," she said with a lift of her aristocratic chin. "And I'm good at my job, so don't get too fond of this place."

Her challenging words roused Mitch's ire, but Collin simply offered her an engaging smile. "I'll see that my grandfather gets the papers."

Hope handed him the folder. "Make sure that you do."

She turned and walked back to her car, opened the door and gracefully slid behind the wheel.

"My, my, my, my, my," Collin said on an exhaled breath. "Did you see those eyes?"

"Collin, she's Jordan's attorney," Mitch reminded him. "She's trying to keep our grandfather from getting this land."

"She doesn't look so tough to me," he replied, watching the car disappear.

"Yeah, well, looks are deceiving."

Collin fingered the manila folder. "Seen the old man lately?"

"A while back he was directing a canopy setup. You might find him behind the house."

Collin headed off and Mitch returned to the twins.

About an hour later cars and trucks started arriving, parking around the house and barns. Guests spilled onto the lawn. Mitch met more of his cousins, talked and joked with his brothers, and kept an eye on the girls.

Summer and Trina arrived together. Trina spotted Mitch and made her way to where he stood wiping watermelon juice from Taylor's arms.

She greeted him warmly. "These are your daughters?"

He nodded. "This is Taylor and this is Ashley. Girls, this is Trina."

"How do you tell them apart?"

He was used to the question from strangers. Oddly enough, Heather had never asked. "Once you get to know them, it's no problem. Ashley's eyes are a little wider. Taylor's chin is narrower."

"I can't see it." She wore a pair of hip-hugging jean shorts and a midriff-baring T-shirt that would have fit his daughters. She leaned down to look into their faces.

Taylor frowned and Mitch held his breath.

"I've been really busy at the Bolton ranch," he said. Why did he feel the need to explain himself to

Trina? He certainly hadn't led her on. Quite the contrary.

She straightened. "I figured that. The job almost finished?"

"A couple more weeks, probably. I'm staying out there, so I haven't been around much."

"I've been staying at home a lot," she said. She glanced at the girls, then leaned close to whisper, "This murder thing has me creeped out."

Mitch had followed some of the details of the murder of Christina Montgomery and the subsequent investigation. "What's happening?" he asked.

"The police arrested Gavin Nighthawk. He's set to stand trial soon. Summer is sure he's innocent. She's beside herself over it. But if it wasn't him, then a killer is still on the loose."

"How does Summer know this Nighthawk guy?"

"She spent summers on the Laughing Horse Reservation where he grew up. Now they're both in residency at Whitehorn Memorial Hospital. I think she's got a thing for him."

Mitch scanned the crowd and found Summer and his grandfather off to the side of the gathering. She seemed agitated and was speaking to him, her hand on his wrist.

As Mitch watched, Garrett gathered her comfortingly against his side and patted her shoulder.

"Mitch!" He turned toward the male voice. Cade was striding toward him, with a couple Mitch had never seen in tow. "Meet my brother, Ryder and his wife, Daisy. They're up from Texas and showing off their new little guy.''

Mitch shook Ryder's hand and admired the baby. Trina asked if she could hold him, and Daisy hovered over them protectively.

Minutes later Garrett announced that food was being served and herded them toward the tables.

Trina quite naturally fell into line with Mitch and his girls, and the four of them ended up on a blanket under a shade tree. From time to time, he scanned the crowd. He hadn't seen Heather arrive, but there were so many cars and such a crowd, he could easily have missed her.

"Will you be here when school starts this fall?" she asked, glancing from Mitch to the twins. "Lynn Garrison is the kindergarten teacher at Whitehorn Elementary. She's really nice. Pretty, too. Her students are crazy about her."

"They went to kindergarten last year," Mitch told her.

"Oh. I probably know the first grade teacher, too. I know several of the teachers, I'm just not sure which grades they teach."

Ashley's plastic cup of lemonade tipped and instantly soaked the seat of Trina's shorts. Trina used the edge of the blanket to blot them dry, and forced a smile.

"I'm gonna get more pickles and some dessert," Ashley said, and took off.

"Garrett picked a great day," Trina commented and Mitch agreed.

Ashley came running back with a precariously tipping paper plate. "I got pie!" She tripped over the edge of the blanket and the piece of cream pie she'd been carrying sailed through the air and landed on Trina's chest, just above the neckline of her shirt. Trina squealed as pudding and banana slices slid inside the fabric.

Sixteen

"Oh!" Taylor immediately went to her sister's aid and scooped the remaining visible pie from Trina's chest into her palm. She didn't make it far before whipped cream and pudding slid between her fingers and dropped on Trina's sandaled foot.

Mitch handed the startled young woman the extra napkins he'd brought along as a habitual precaution. She used a couple to unsuccessfully wipe cream pie from her chest, reaching inside her shirt to wipe out more. Watching her try to clean herself, Mitch struggled to suppress the laugh that surged up toward his throat. He forced it down and worked on the gooey stuff between her toes.

With a perplexed expression, Trina plucked her shirt away from her skin and gestured that the napkin attempt was futile.

"I, uh…" He cleared his throat and started over. "I'll show you where the bathroom is. You can wash up in there." He turned to his daughters and pointed threateningly. "Don't either one of you move a muscle."

In seeming wide-eyed innocence, they shook their heads.

Mitch felt dozens of eyes on them as they crossed the lawn to the house. He held the door open for her and led the way to the bathroom off the kitchen. "I'll run up and get you a clean shirt," he said, and ran up the stairs to the room that still held a few drawers of his clothing.

Locating one of his smallest polo shirts, he hurried down and tapped on the bathroom door.

"Mitch? Come in."

Hesitantly he opened the door. She stood facing the sink, with her slender naked back to him as she washed out her T-shirt. Uh-uh. He wasn't going to get mixed up in a new situation. Immediately he averted his gaze and draped the clean shirt over a wooden cabinet right inside. "Here."

"Thanks."

He backed out and closed the door. In the kitchen, he wet a dishtowel and carried it outdoors.

"Now can I go get a new piece of pie?" Ashley asked.

He wiped her hands, then Taylor's. "You will tell Trina you're sorry when she comes back."

"I din't mean to drop my pie on her!"

"You still need to apologize for the accident."

Ashley pouted. "Awright."

"Okay, you two may go get pie. But this time *walk* back with it."

Mitch did his best to clean off the blanket, then gave up and turned it over.

"Look, Daddy!" Taylor called to him.

Mitch glanced up and discovered Heather and her children walking toward him with his daughters.

"Hi," he said.

Heather shifted Andrew on her hip. "Hi."

"Have you eaten?" he asked.

She nodded. "My kids wouldn't touch the barbe-cued pork, though."

He grinned. "Mine neither."

"There's a whole corner of Garrett's lawn over there covered with Andrew's chips."

"Banana cream pie and pickles," Mitch replied, pointing to the pile of napkins on his plate on the ground.

Heather laughed.

Her gaze moved to someone approaching.

Trina came up beside Mitch. His shirt was way too large for her, but she'd tied a knot at her waist, never one to allow too much skin to be covered at once, he noted. The soft cotton draped and outlined her small breasts. He should have given her a flannel shirt.

Mitch met Heather's eyes. She'd seen the direction of his gaze, and he felt his skin grow hot.

Trina hooked a finger in Mitch's belt loop, play-fully, possessively. "Hi," she said to Heather.

Andrew leaned forward so fast that Heather had to catch him. He stretched his chubby arms toward Mitch.

Mitch took him, forcing Trina to let go. "Heather Johnson, this is Trina McCann."

The two exchanged a cool greeting.

Trina stared at the boy who'd latched on to Mitch, then glanced around at the throng of children.

"Let's go play croquet," Taylor suggested.

"You be careful with those mallets," Mitch warned as the twins and Heather's two older children trotted off. "And keep the balls on the ground." He emphasized the final words with a stern expression.

"We will!" they called back amid squeals of laughter.

Ashley hadn't apologized to Trina.

The three adults glanced at each other uncomfortably.

"Heather's ranch is the Bolton ranch where I'm working," Mitch said finally.

Trina nodded. "Oh." And from that information she knew that was where he was staying, too.

"I think I'll go keep an eye on the kids," Heather said. She reached for Andrew, but he clung to Mitch's shirt. Mitch had to open the toddler's fisted hands to loosen him. He puckered up to cry.

Heather kissed his forehead. "It's all right. We'll go watch the kids play ball."

"Ball?" he echoed.

She gave a little wave and walked away. Mitch watched her go. Turning, he found Trina studying him. "Nice lady," she said.

"Yes."

"Pretty, too."

"Uh-huh. Trina, let's go for a walk."

"Sure."

He led her aside, beneath the sun-filtering leaves of one of the aged trees, and along a pasture fence where wild daisies grew in profusion. He considered his words carefully. He'd thought he'd made himself clear the last time, but apparently he hadn't.

"Trina, I don't know how to say this any other way." He paused, then went on. "There can't be anything between us. Not now and not later. It's not that I don't think you're nice or pretty or any of that. It's just that it's not there."

She studied his face for a moment, then glanced toward the mountains. "I know."

That hammered him. He stumbled on a clump of grass and caught himself. "You do?"

She nodded and gestured back toward the ranch house. "It's her, isn't it?"

"She's part of it," he replied honestly.

"The other stuff is the rest of it."

"What other stuff?"

She made a face.

"The girls?" he prompted.

"Kind of." She released a pent-up breath. "It's not that I don't like them. But they've been with you for a long time. You're already a family together, the three of you. I want to make my own family."

Didn't that beat all? Didn't that just beat all? "That's perfectly understandable."

She placed her hand on his arm. "If we can't have a casual relationship, then I think we should just be friends," she said.

He raised a brow.

"You can't blame a girl for trying," she said on a laugh.

Relief swept over him and he smiled. "No."

She reached up on tiptoe to kiss his cheek.

"Want to try another piece of pie?" he asked.

"She did that deliberately, didn't she?"

He couldn't help chuckling as he led her back toward the gathering and the food tables.

One of his other half brothers, Adam Benson, passed Mitch with a plate and a mug of beer. "Hey, Mitch! Victoria is over here. Come say hi."

Mitch joined him and his other half brothers and their wives, and enjoyed the conversation and the banter.

Before long, Garrett announced games, and three-legged runs and barrel races began. Later, while the girls were occupied in a supervised game, he joined a small gathering of men, including Cade, Ryder, and Collin, and listened attentively to their talk of horses and ranch management. It wasn't farfetched to imagine himself as a rancher. The idea appealed to him more and more all the time, and the girls were thriving here.

He wasn't going to set his hopes on the land Garrett wanted to give him, since the situation with Jordan and Hope Baxter was up in the air. But he could build up his business here and buy his own land. He had some insurance money he'd invested, if he decided to make a purchase. The idea instantly became more tangible.

Sunset arrived in myriad vibrant oranges and streaks of lavender, and the air cooled. From the corner of his eye, Mitch caught site of Heather's pewter Blazer winding away from the ranch. She probably felt safer driving on the mountains roads before full dark, but standing in the midst of all these people, Mitch felt lonelier than he'd ever felt before.

He half listened to the conversation around him. How was it that Heather Johnson had become such a force that his well-being seemed to revolve around her presence? He'd done that to himself—allowed her to become too important, allowed his feelings for her to override common sense. She wanted nothing from him except a few pleasant physical encounters.

The knowledge hurt.

Maybe once Heather was gone, he would be able to get his emotions back on an even keel, look for a woman ready for a relationship, one without all the scars and baggage.

It grew dark and he gathered the girls and told Garrett goodbye. Exhausted, the twins fell asleep nearly as soon as he headed down the drive.

He'd gone about five miles, when up ahead, the rhythmic flashing of a vehicle's emergency lights could be seen through the trees. Mitch slowed and rounded the curve. He pulled to the side, the Silverado's headlights gleaming across the back end and bumper of a Blazer—his heart skipped—Heather's Blazer.

The front end of her vehicle was tilted down off the side of the road.

Mitch parked, jumped out and ran forward.

The driver's door opened and Heather, looking a bit shaken, stepped out.

"What happened?" he asked, taking her by her elbows and feeling her trembling.

She clasped his forearms and clung to him, her shaky voice belying her words. "It's nothing, really. A tire blew. The front right one."

He noticed a scrape above her eyebrow, along with a slight swelling that concerned him. "Are you all right?"

She touched the spot gingerly, then looked at her fingers. "Why didn't the air bags inflate?"

"The sensor for them is in the front bumper. You didn't hit anything."

"The car jerked off to the right and over the edge of the road. The steering wheel was yanked right out of my control."

Mitch released Heather to open the back door. Three wide sets of eyes stared at him apprehensively. Wet trails on Patrick's and Andrew's cheeks showed they'd been crying. All of them remained buckled into their restraints, Andrew in his car seat. "You guys all right?"

Jessica and Patrick nodded. Andrew stretched his arms toward Mitch.

Mitch leaned in the door and gave them each a comforting touch on the head. "We'll get you out of here and you'll be home in no time, okay?"

"No tine," Andrew said seriously.

"Right." He figured out how to unbuckle Andrew and his car seat and carried both to his truck. Heather helped Jessica and Patrick out.

It took several minutes to make room for the car seat and to situate the children in his pickup. Taylor roused and asked what was going on.

"The Johnsons are going to sit with you for a while. You can go back to sleep." He backed out and said to Heather, "They're fine. Shut the doors or the mosquitoes will eat 'em alive." He nodded toward her pickup. "You do have a spare under there."

"Yes."

He got into his lockbox for tools and a tow chain.

"I don't think I can jack up that front end the way it's sitting. We're going to have to pull it back up first."

"That's why I didn't try it," she said with a nod. "What do you want me to do?"

"Are you feeling all right?"

"Just a little shaken up is all."

"You're sure?"

"I'm sure."

"Sit behind the wheel, and put your seat belt on. Shift into Neutral, and when I have you up here, move it into Park."

She nodded and got into the vehicle.

He got in his truck, where Taylor had draped her arm across Andrew, giving him the comfort he'd needed to fall asleep already. Mitch assured Jessica and Patrick that everything was fine, and shifted into gear.

He got the Blazer onto the road, unbolted the spare from its rack beneath the frame, then quickly changed the tire.

Someone would have come along if it hadn't been him, Mitch reasoned, but his thoughts shifted to Trina's concern over a murderer on the loose in the county. He was grateful Heather wasn't alone at her ranch.

They paused for a moment. "The kids are all settled in there now," he said. "I don't want you to drive. Ride home with me, and we'll come get the Blazer tomorrow."

She touched her head and glanced into the truck, obviously thinking of the safety of her children.

"Get in," he said decisively. "I'll pull the Blazer off the road."

"Get my purse, please."

Mitch and Heather rode with Jessica between them in the front. Jessica took her mother's hand and held it.

"I promised you we'd go riding tomorrow morning, and we're still going to do it," Heather told her.

"Can the twins sleep with you tonight, Jess?" Mitch asked.

She nodded. "Sure."

"I'll stay downstairs on the couch, so I can check on your mom every so often."

"I'm fine," Heather objected.

He didn't argue with her, just drove to the ranch. "Clean that cut while I get the kids ready for bed."

"But I—"

"They see you in the light and they'll be scared. Just go."

Heather's head was pounding, whether from stress or the bump or both, she didn't know. In the upstairs bathroom she glanced in the mirror and saw the dried blood and slight swelling that Mitch hadn't wanted the kids to see. She washed her face and blotted her bruised eyebrow.

She took the first-aid kit into her bedroom and dotted tincture of iodine on the cut and placed an adhesive strip over it. Finding a bottle of aspirin, she took two and changed into her nightshirt and robe.

A soft knock alerted her to Mitch's presence in the doorway. "The kids are all asleep."

"Thanks, Mitch."

"Are you dizzy or anything?" he asked, concern etching his features.

She declared she was fine.

"Get some rest. I'll come check on you later."

"I'll be fine."

"I know you will. But I'll check on you anyway."

She drank in the sight of him, standing with one hand on the door frame, his hips cocked in a decidedly masculine pose. She needed him to come close.

To touch her and offer reassurance and comfort as he had the children. She really was fine. No one had been hurt and her little bump didn't amount to anything. But it had been a terrible scare. His strong arms around her would feel so good right now.

It was unfair of her to want anything from him. It had been unfair of her to allow their attraction to go as far as it had. She'd been selfish.

His gaze touched on her robe, her bare feet, the bed.

Erotic memories of their night together in this room rose up to envelop her.

Seventeen

"Holler if you need anything," Mitch said. He started to back out of the room.

"Mitch?"

He paused. "Yeah?"

Loneliness created an ache she'd learned to live with until now. She'd allowed herself to be vulnerable to the pain again. "There are blankets and pillows in that closet at the top of the stairs."

He nodded, turned and left.

Heather removed her robe, doused the light, and climbed into bed. Her shoulders and arms ached, and she worked at relaxing them.

She wasn't dependent on a man. Anyone alone on that road in the same situation would have needed a tow out of the ditch. Her calmness had been mostly bravado for the children's sake, and seeing Mitch's truck appear had given her a genuine sense of relief.

He would have been kind and concerned about anyone, but it warmed her to think he'd been especially concerned because it had been her and her family stranded on that road. She didn't want him to care that much, though, and she couldn't afford the guilt that went with hoping he did.

Heather rolled onto her side and hugged a pillow to her breast. She'd been self-conscious attending Garrett's party after being away from Whitehorn so long. But everyone had been friendly and welcoming, and she hadn't felt like an outsider at all.

At least not until she'd seen Mitch with the lovely young blonde. It had been impossible to not notice that she was enamored with Mitch.

She was the sort of girl he'd be better off with. If he could be happy with her, Heather would be happy for him.

But seeing them together bothered her.

Oh, it bothered her.

She couldn't look at him without remembering his touches. His kisses. She couldn't watch the shapely blonde lingering near him without wondering if Mitch would touch her in the same ways, kiss her in the same places.

When had she become preoccupied with musings like these? What invading force had taken over her mind and senses and impelled her to think disturbing sensual thoughts?

She wasn't supposed to care. Caring too much, letting him get too close, would start to chip away little pieces of the new person she'd worked so hard to become.

He was downstairs on the couch right now. All the kids were asleep. All she had to do was go down there and avail herself to the comfort and pleasure of being with him. Or could she? He'd made himself scarce the past several days. He'd tuned into his survival instincts and started construction on a sturdy wall between them. At this point, could it be breached?

If she went down, would he even give in to another night? It wouldn't be fair to ask him. Nothing had changed.

She was still heading back to California once the ranch was ready to sell. If she stayed much longer, she wouldn't be able to go. She'd be a prisoner again. But, then, why did she have to stay?

Heather thought the situation over. She had gone through all of the personal items in her father's study and left only important documents, like registration papers for the horses and deeds and warranties.

She given his clothing to the Stop-n-Swap, and the closets were empty of all but their things. The house could be shown with only the furniture remaining.

She could head out by next week. Mitch could finish the work without her here. He would have to figure out what to do with the twins, but something could probably be arranged.

She'd been procrastinating, drawing out her stay, and she knew it. She'd enjoyed her days and evenings with the children, their walks together, their slow-paced summer routine, her newfound ability to bend with situations. But it was time to get back to reality. Time to head out before she gave up her independence.

Sleep finally came for her, and she slipped into its uneasy arms.

* * *

She awoke rested the following morning, her head-ache gone, with vague memories of Mitch's quiet checks during the night. She showered and dressed and discovered the kids's rooms empty.

They were all in the kitchen, the mouth-watering smell of cinnamon and syrup in the air.

He'd prepared a mountain of French toast, and two stacks still remained in the center of the table.

"How's your head, Mom?" Jessica asked, frowning at the bandage and the faintly bruised area around Heather's eye. She got up, poured Heather a glass of orange juice and brought it to her where she'd seated herself at the end of the table.

"Thank you, darling." She took a refreshing sip. "My head's just fine."

"Ouchie!" Andrew called, pointing at his mother.

"A little ouchie," she replied. "Mommy's okay."

Mitch was picking globs of French toast out of the baby's hair.

"Are we still on for this morning?" she asked him.

He went and rinsed his hands at the sink. "I'm here. Eat your breakfast and, as long as you're feeling up to it, head on out for your ride."

Jessica jumped up and down in excitement. "Yes!"

"I wanna ride, too," Patrick said with a sticky-looking pout.

"Me, too!"

"Me, too!" Taylor and Ashley chimed in simul-taneously.

"Not this time," Mitch said firmly. "This morning is just for Heather and Jessica. We'll have to stay home and do something boring, like...bake cookies...or catch a pigeon in the barn."

"A pigeon!" Patrick shouted. "Hey, cool! Can I keep 'im?"

Heather ate, then stood and stopped abruptly. "I don't have any way to get over there."

Mitch reached into his pocket and handed her his keys. "Take mine. We'll go get your Blazer when you get back."

She thanked him and she and Jess headed out the door.

Their neighbor, Martin Rollins, had known her father for years, remembered her mother, too, and told Heather he wanted to show her something. She'd just arrived and knocked at the back door when he pulled her into the kitchen.

His wife, Ella, smiled at the two of them. "What a pretty young daughter you have."

"Why, thank you."

"Here it is," Martin said. He wore his dark denim jeans loose, with the cuffs rolled atop his boots. His skin was sun-darkened and lined, his faded blue eyes kind. He held a black-and-white photograph toward Heather.

She accepted it and studied the picture. It was her as a child of perhaps eight or nine. She wore a dress with a white collar, chaps, and boots. She sat atop a bay, a pretty horse with a white diamond on her forehead. In front of them, holding the reins, was her father.

An elusive image flitted through her memory, the image of her father helping her onto the horse and smiling up at her, squinting in the sun.

"Let me see, Mom." Jessica stood on tiptoe, so Heather lowered the photograph. "Is this you? Your hair sure was weird."

"Thanks."

"Is this Grandpa?"

"That's him."

"Did he take you riding?"

"Sometimes. When I was small."

"He was a broken man after your mama died," Martin said with a shake of his head. Thin gray hair covered his tanned scalp in combed streaks.

Heather tried to hand the picture back, but he shoved it toward her. "You keep it. It'll just get lost in the jumble when we pass on."

"Thanks. I'll leave it here until we're done riding."

He walked outside with them. "All the horses in that north pasture are yours. I took what feed and hay was left in your barns. Makes it easier for me to keep them here. Hope you don't mind."

"Not at all. I'm sure I owe you something for their keep. Vet bills, that kind of thing." She lowered the tailgate and took down a saddle.

Martin got the other one. "I have some receipts,

but it's not much. Have you decided what to do with the horses yet? You want to auction 'em?''

"That would probably bring me the best price, wouldn't it?'' She studied the horses grazing in the sloping pasture. Several ran gracefully toward a stand of trees on the hill. She'd forgotten how beautiful they were. She turned to him. "You want any of them?''

He studied the animals. "Well...''

"I'd be glad to trade for their keep and the vet bills.''

"Maybe one or two. I'm not gonna rob, ya, missy. You got some fine horseflesh there.'' They walked toward the stable with the saddles. "My man, Lefty, brought a couple mares inside for you.''

She thanked the wiry ranch hand who hefted a saddle onto the back of a spotted horse for her. Martin lifted the other one.

Heather rubbed the horse's forehead and spoke to her softly. She fastened her saddle and harnesses, while Martin did the other one, explaining to Jessica what he was doing. Heather double-checked all the straps and buckles on both saddles, then helped Jessica up. Martin handed her the reins.

"These my father's horses, too?'' Heather asked as she placed a foot in the stirrup and swung up.

"Yup.''

The mare's head, neck and forelegs were gleaming black, her rump leopard-spotted with white and gray. "What breed is she?''

"Rangerbred is what I'd call her. Your pa claimed

they're Colorado Rangers. They're Turkish Arabians of some sort. He'd have papers for them. They're the best of his stock.''

"There are registration papers in his safe," she said with a nod. She guided the horse out of the stable and Jess's mount followed. "We're going to start out in the corral this morning," she told her daughter.

"Ah, Mom."

"Don't 'Ah, Mom' me. We don't know these animals and I haven't ridden for a long, long time."

"I have!"

She laughed. "Those pony rides at the zoo don't count."

After a half hour of getting used to their seat and gait in the corral, she led them out and into a pasture.

Jessica had a ball, and Heather rediscovered her love of riding. She had the wild desire to break out of the fenced-in space and ride as fast and far as the mount would take her. She remembered the wind in her hair, the thrill of the ride...the freedom.

Jess galloped up beside her and the expression of joy on her lovely young face took Heather's breath away. Occasionally Jess reminded Heather of Craig, but most of the time she saw simply the unique girl she loved with all her heart. Today, the resemblance to herself, to the girl in that black-and-white photo was strong.

What kind of memories would Jessica carry into her adult life? She hoped only the ones of days such as this—the good times they'd shared. Their good times would be more plentiful than a singular long-forgotten day captured in a photograph.

Soon enough the sun was high and she took Jess back to the stable and showed her how to rub down and groom the horse properly. It struck Heather then that today was a memory for her, as well. Slowly, the ugly memories of Montana were being overshadowed by pleasant ones.

The realization reassured and frightened her at the same time. She needed to leave. She didn't want to have any regrets.

"Can we ride again, Mom? Maybe we can come tomorrow."

Heather lifted a saddle, her shoulder aching, and got it as far as a stool. She studied her lovely daughter's animated face. "Well. Maybe just once or twice more before we leave."

Maybe a few more good memories to take back.

"Wouldn't it be cool if we brought a couple horses home with us?"

Heather blinked at her. "To San Francisco? Sweetie, it would cost a fortune to board them."

Jessica got an odd look on her face and glanced away. "Well, no. I kind of meant back to the ranch."

Her daughter's words sunk in with surprise. *Wouldn't it be cool if we brought a couple horses home with us?* And she remembered Mitch's words the night before. *We'll get you out of here and you'll be home in no time, okay?*

Mitch and the kids thought of the ranch as home.

Eighteen

Surely it was just a figure of speech.

Mitch had never spoken of where he'd lived before, or since his wife's death. He'd spoken of his mother and mother-in-law caring for the girls while he worked. He'd been perfectly at ease with bringing their belongings to the bunkhouse and living there.

What did "home" truly mean?

Her kids had nice rooms in their city apartment. Of course, they spent most of their days in day care and school, their family time occupied with Heather cooking and cleaning and doing laundry for the next day. Planning ahead and keeping an agenda was the only way to survive her job and her kids.

Since the demands on her time and her performance had been eased here at the ranch, she'd become less structured and more lenient. Lenient with the kids. Lenient with herself.

And they'd all benefited. No wonder the kids liked it here. No wonder Jessica referred to the ranch as home.

Heather would miss this. All of this.

She would miss the kids more than ever when she

went back to work. To a job that could get by without her.

She instructed Martin to cut a couple of horses for his own herd, thanked him and drove Mitch's truck back to her ranch. The thought of going back to California and never seeing Mitch again created an ache in her heart. She would just have to deal with it.

Once Heather had parked and she and Jess got out of the truck, the sound of hammering caught their attention. They followed it to the bunkhouse.

An odd sight greeted them. The inflatable pool had been blown up inside, and within its confines sat Andrew, contentedly playing with a stack of freshly made wooden blocks, safely sanded, but void of paint or decoration. He seemed to not care, stacking them and knocking them down.

The twins and Patrick were engrossed in a board game at the trestle table. A bowl of popcorn sat between them, the scarred floor scattered with kernels that had missed their mouths.

Mitch was humming to himself and hanging doors on shelves he'd constructed on the wall beside the sink. Those slim-fitting jeans and that tool belt were a combination guaranteed to draw Heather's appreciative gaze to his hips.

"Mommy!" Patrick spotted her and climbed down from his chair to give her a hug.

She hugged him soundly, and he went back to his game.

Jessica joined them. Mitch turned and gave her a smile. "How's the head?"

"I'd forgotten all about it."

"Good. Got a hand to lend me?"

"Sure."

"Could you hold this in place for a minute?"

She held a cabinet door while he aligned the hinges and placed the screws in the wood.

"How was your ride?"

She smiled. "Great. I'd forgotten how much I enjoyed it."

"Jess liked it?"

"Loved it. She had a ball. Very clever of you to occupy the darlings so you could get a little work in. The pool was sheer genius."

"Wasn't it?" He grinned. "I'm learning. You can let go."

She stepped away.

He brushed his hands off on his thighs. "I'm going to finish this and clean up, then we'll go get the Blazer."

"Okay."

"Since you'll almost be there, will you join me for dinner at Garrett's?"

"Oh, I don't think so, Mitch. I wouldn't want to impose."

"It's not an imposition. Family and friends always drop by on Sundays. He plans for a crowd, and he loves every minute of it."

"No, really," she said. "I wouldn't feel right."

"Okay." He shrugged and bent to place his tools in his toolbox. He hadn't expected her to accept, really, but he didn't want her to be alone if she'd rather have company. From a crouched position, he glanced up at her. "Would you rather I didn't go? I don't mind staying, if you think you'll need some rest or something."

"Is that what this is about? No, I told you I'm fine. You go have your dinner like you usually do."

She took the kids outdoors and left Mitch to grab a quick shower. He hadn't slept well on her couch last night. He'd ventured up to check on her every hour or so. Usually she'd slept right through his visit to her room, but once she'd roused with a sigh and reached for him. He'd given her his hand and she'd pulled it to her face for a moment, rubbed her soft cheek against his fingers, then held his palm against her breast until she fell soundly asleep.

He was determined to separate himself from the temptation she presented, but this incident had interrupted his plan. She didn't have anyone else, and she seemed particularly vulnerable right now. As self-sufficient and capable as she was, circumstances made everyone need a little help from time to time.

Mitch dressed and called the twins in to wash, and he changed them into clean clothes. In a matter of minutes they were all settled in his crew cab.

"This road is probably treacherous in the winter," Mitch commented as they neared the spot where they'd left the Blazer.

"Why's that?" Jessica asked.

"Snow and ice would make these mountain roads dangerous."

"There's snow in Montana?" she asked.

Mitch nodded.

Patrick leaned forward and peered out the window. "Where's snow?"

Mitch laughed. "There's no snow right now except up on the mountains, but at Christmastime there'll be lots of snow down here."

"Can we see it?" Patrick asked excitedly. "Can we, Mom?"

"We'll be back in California long before that," was her reply.

"Aw," Patrick groaned. "I want to stay and see the snow."

From the corner of his eye Mitch caught Jess glancing at her mother. "Maybe we can visit," she said hopefully.

Heather made no reply.

"Can you ride horses in the winter?" the girl asked, this time directing her query to Mitch.

"Sure," Mitch replied. "Used to be the only way to get around, before there were cars and four-wheel-drive vehicles."

"Cool," she said.

Mitch spotted the Blazer and pulled off the road in front of it. He got out to assist, transferring Andrew's car seat. The little boy raised his chubby arms to Mitch and Mitch took him for a hug before placing him in his seat and fastening the restraints. Andrew puckered up and cried broken-heartedly.

"I'll see you later, buddy," he told him with a wave.

Heather thanked him and got into her vehicle. He waited until she got it started and headed back toward her ranch.

"Seems kinda lonesome when they leave, don't it?" Ashley asked with six-year-old guilelessness and sixty-year-old insight.

"We've still got each other," Mitch told her.

He looked over his shoulder to see that Taylor had taken her sister's hand and held it in silent consolation. *There* were those darling angelic babies he'd first known. His chest ached with love and a desire to give them what they needed most. He wanted them to feel part of a family so badly he could taste it.

Because he'd felt out of place with his stepsiblings, he'd craved a true family of his own. His marriage to Jamie and the birth of their girls had given him the family he'd missed out on.

And then that family had been broken by her death. His girls deserved a full measure. He deserved it, too.

"I love you guys," he said around a lump in his throat.

"Love you, Daddy," they chorused.

"Summer's asked me to go talk with Gavin Night-hawk," Garrett was filling Mitch in as they waited in the study for Hattie to announce dinner.

"In jail?" Mitch asked.

"She is convinced he's innocent and has asked me to do something."

"What can you do?"

"If I believe his story, I can hire a decent attorney for him."

"And you'd be willing to do that?"

"I'd do it for Summer."

"It's really important to her, huh?"

Garrett nodded affirmatively. "I'm famished. Hope the others get here soon."

"It's pretty quiet. I think I'd better check on the twins."

Mitch found the girls in the hallway, where they'd created a tent out of an antique table and a fringed tablecloth. "Come out from under there. Did you ask permission to play here? I don't think it's such a good idea."

He smoothed the tablecloth back into its original position. "It's almost time to eat."

The girls took his hands. On the way past a long polished table, Taylor reached for a tin of chocolates.

"Whoa, there," Mitch said, intercepting the piece of candy. "You guys haven't eaten your dinner yet."

"Don't want dinner," Taylor pouted. "Want candy."

"Well, you're not getting any until I say so. You'd be bouncing of the walls if I let you eat this now."

"You're mean!"

"I'm sorry you think that," he said, borrowing a

line he'd heard Heather use. "But those are the rules."

Taylor and Ashley exchanged a look. Dad holding firm on this rule stuff was still a novelty. "What about after dinner?" Ashley asked.

"After dinner you can each have a couple."

Taylor held up three fingers. "This many?"

"Two," he replied.

She scowled.

Mitch held firm and hid the tin of candy on top of an armoire.

"Daddy won't let us eat the chocolates until after supper," Ashley told her great-grandfather.

"Well, that sounds fair to me." Garrett patted the cushion of the leather sofa where he sat. "Dads know best, you know."

Ashley seated herself primly beside him.

"Daddy, don't Patrick and them guys know what snow looks like?" Ashley asked.

"No," he replied. "There's no snow where they live."

"Not even in winter?"

"Not even in winter."

"Gosh."

"Cade and Leanne aren't coming today?" Mitch asked his grandfather.

"They're doing something with Cade's brother to-day."

Mitch's half brother, Blake Remmington, and his wife, Serena, and their son, Nate, arrived then.

"Look at this future rancher," Garrett said, admiring his handsome great-grandson.

The girls had someone new to pay attention to. The boy was near the same age, with straight dark hair like his mother and blue eyes like his father. The three entertained a lively conversation.

Dinner was announced, and they all moved into the dining room.

"Aren't they a lovely family?" Garrett said to Mitch, referring to Blake and Serena.

"Yes," Mitch agreed. Nobody missed having a complete family more than Mitch.

While the others visited, Garrett leaned close to Mitch and said quietly, "Have you thought any more about staying?"

Nineteen

Mitch knew his grandfather was referring to his staying in Whitehorn permanently. "Sure have. Haven't decided anything though."

Disappointment was apparent in the droop of Garrett's shoulders. He raised a brow. "There's plenty of young women in Whitehorn."

Mitch stopped him. "Please don't fix me up with anyone else. I appreciate the effort—and the thought, but if I'm going to meet someone, I'd rather do it on my own."

"You're hankerin' after that Johnson woman, aren't you?"

"And if I was?"

"Way I understand it, she's planning on heading back to California. Is that right?"

"She has a good job in San Francisco."

Garrett studied Mitch's face, and Mitch put on his best mask of unconcern, wondering if the old man was fooled.

"There's land here for you, son. Land that's rightfully yours."

"That's generous of you, and I promise to deal with that if the time comes."

"*When* the time comes," Garrett said forcefully.

They shared a look, and Mitch felt bad about not sharing his thoughts with someone who obviously cared so much. "Okay, I'm thinking really strongly that I'd like to stay here. There are more reasons to stay than to go. But I don't want to say for sure. Nobody should get their hopes up yet, not you and not the girls. Not until I decide."

Or not until Heather was really gone and he had to focus on the rest of his life without her.

"I respect that you want time to decide what you want," the old man said. "You need that. I'm not a meddling old fool. I just want you here. Too selfishly, I guess."

"You're not selfish." Mitch grinned and finished his dinner.

It was early evening when the Fielding trio arrived back at the Bolton ranch. The girls asked if they could go spend a few minutes with Jessica.

"Go ahead. But if they're doing a family thing, come right back."

"Like what?" Taylor asked.

"Like watching a video or playing a game together or something."

"That's family things?" she questioned.

"Sort of."

"How will we know?" Ashley was wondering now.

"Never mind." He waved them toward the door. "Knock!"

"Jess sees me, Dad. She's right there at the table." Taylor opened the screen door and walked in, Ashley on her heels.

Mitch stood studying the new porch and eaves, noticing a place that needed touching up.

A few minutes later the back door opened and the girls filed out. "Can Jess come over and play with us, Daddy? Her mom's upstairs with the boys."

"If it's okay with her mom."

"It is," Jessica said. "I already asked her."

He walked behind them to the bunkhouse, listening in amusement to their girlish chatter. Once inside they gathered brushes and combs and a mirror and turned the table into a beauty parlor.

Mitch changed out of his good slacks and set about finishing the built-ins he'd started that morning.

Jessica's words stopped him. "We're going back to San Francisco."

"Not for a long time," Taylor said.

"Yuh-huh," Jess informed her. "My mom said at the end of this week we're goin'. She's gonna have Mr. Rollins sell our horses, and the house-seller lady is coming tomorrow."

But the work's not finished, Mitch wanted to shout. There were still at least three weeks of work left to remodel the upstairs bath and the kitchen. The outbuildings needed painting, too. He gripped his hammer and listened to the girls's talk turn serious.

"I wish we could stay," Jessica told the twins. "I asked my mom, but she said this can't be our home.

She has her job and I have my school. Patrick will go to school this year, too.''

''We might get to go to school here in Montana,'' Ashley said. ''We hope so, anyway. You could go to school here, too.''

''I know. But my mom said we can't stay.''

''I think I'm gonna cry,'' Taylor announced.

Jess and Ashley patted her back.

Mitch knew how she felt. They were leaving. It was real. Definite. Heather'd never led him to believe any differently. What had he imagined? That she'd fall so hard for him, she'd change all her plans and give up her job and change her life just for him? Yeah, right.

He finished the cabinets and sanded them with less enthusiasm than he'd begun the project. The wood needed a sealer, but he didn't want to release the chemical smell just before they'd be going to bed. He put away his supplies and told the girls it was time to get ready for bed. Standing on the porch, he watched Jess return to the house and turn with a forlorn wave.

He waved back.

He bathed the girls, read them a story and put them to bed. ''Can me an' Taylor sleep together tonight, Daddy?'' Ashley asked.

He understood the comfort they needed, and was glad they could give it to each other. ''Sure. It's crowded, but I guess you don't care.''

Taylor climbed out of the covers and into his lap. With a sweet ache in his chest, he returned her hug, enjoying her baby-fresh smell. He'd buckled down on the rules, disciplined them because he loved them. And for the first time he could remember, Taylor was seeking affection in his arms.

"'Night, Daddy."

"'Night, sweetheart. Know how much I love you?"

"How much?"

"As much as there is snow in the mountains."

"Wow!"

"Me, too?" Ashley asked. "How much do you love me?"

He tucked Taylor back in and spoke to his other daughter. "I love you as much as there is water in the ocean."

"Is that a lot?"

"It's a whole lot."

"Maybe we can go visit Jess and the boys sometime and see."

He kissed their foreheads and turned off the wall lamp. "Maybe we can."

He closed the door. Finding a stack of carpentry magazines he'd set aside to read, he grabbed a cola and settled into the only comfortable chair. He'd been distractedly reading for half an hour when a light knock sounded on the door.

Heather stood on the other side of the screen. "Can I come in for a few minutes?"

"Sure." He stood back and let her pass into the room.

She sat on one of the ancient rockers.

"Want something to drink?"

"No thanks."

He went back to his chair.

"I'm leaving at the end of the week."

"So I heard."

She looked a little embarrassed. "Oh. Jess told you?"

"She told the girls."

"Sorry you had to find out like that."

He leaned forward. "What about the sale of the house?"

"The Realtor can do it now. It's almost ready. She can send any papers I need to sign by FedEx service. I've got nearly everything done that I needed to do."

He studied her without comment, his heart being torn in two.

"I'm sorry about the girls. I'll help you find someone to watch them."

"I can do it."

"I feel responsible."

"You're not responsible for my daughters."

Her expression shuttered and her gaze lowered. She flattened her hands on her knees. "Okay." She studied the backs of her ringless fingers. "I think some of the horses are going to pull a good price. I'll be able to pay you as soon as they're sold."

"Our agreement was that we'd settle after the sale of the ranch."

"This will be faster."

"I'm not destitute."

"I want to pay the debt. You did the work."

"The work's not finished."

"I know, but—"

"I found something out for you," he said.

She met his eyes at last. "What's that?"

"That tractor you have out there is worth a few thousand dollars. That's one of the first tractors made when they switched over from horses. And it's in excellent shape."

"Great."

"I checked around because I didn't want someone to take advantage of you."

"Thanks. I wouldn't have known."

He waved away her thanks, torn between wanting her to leave if she was going to leave and wanting to prolong their time together.

She stood, ending his dilemma.

He wished she would take the few steps to reach him and touch him. Touch his hair maybe. His face. Give him few more kisses to last him a lifetime. Fill his head with the scent of her.

She was either strong-willed or leaving him wasn't tearing her apart the way it was him. The time spent in each other's arms meant nothing to her. He meant nothing to her.

He could ask her to talk to him, but she would say the same things she had before. He could ask her to stay and make a bigger fool of himself. He stood.

"Well, that's it, then." She turned toward the door. "'Night."

"'Night." The door opened and closed. She was gone.

Mitch stood watching the darkness beyond the screen. He walked onto the porch, but she was already gone from sight.

Twenty

Mitch had moved the refrigerator and the microwave into the laundry room temporarily, while the kitchen was under construction. Meals would have to be simple, and trips to the café would be in order for that week.

On Monday morning Mitch and his crew tore out the old plaster walls and hung the vinyl wallpaper-look-alike paneling that Heather had selected in Billings. Mitch spent the next two days installing new cupboards and the dishwasher and range. Subcontractors handled the electrical and plumbing throughout, while his crew kept up with the touch-up work and laid a tile floor.

He worked from morning to night with minimal breaks for food and water. At noon each day he used the phone in the study, telling Heather he'd pay for the calls he was making.

"I've found a nanny for the girls," he announced on Thursday afternoon. Heather was cleaning out the refrigerator, which was still operational and not that old. Her father must have replaced it out of necessity within the last few years.

"You did?"

"She can't get here for another week. She's coming from Germany."

"A few of my co-workers have had nannies from other countries," she said. "Seems they change them often. Does this one speak English?"

"I understood her fairly well on the phone," he said. "She has good references."

"What will you do until she gets here?"

"My sister-in-law Leanne has agreed to help me until then."

"Well, that's good."

"Yep." That said, he went back to work.

Their conversation had been at a bare minimum all week, but then, the remodeling had created chaos, and no one wanted to see it finished more than she did.

Thursday night, sitting alone in the nearly finished kitchen, Heather imagined a family gathering in the new room for hectic meals and cozy evenings. She hoped someone with children would move in. It was a great place for kids.

The phone rang and she picked it up.

"I know it's late," the woman from the realty company said. "But we have an offer."

Heather's heart pounded. "Already?"

"The party's been interested in the land for some time. It's a substantial offer. I think you should consider it."

"Well, of course I will." She listened to the woman and the offer and hung up the phone with completely torn feelings. This was what she'd wanted, what she'd worked toward. The offer would more than cover the contracting, pay Mitch, and give her something to invest. She could even buy a house in San Francisco if she wanted to.

She walked through the house, seeing the improvements she and Mitch had made together. Except for the old furnishings, it looked nothing like the house of her childhood, nothing like the place where those bad memories of Montana had been carved.

Everywhere she looked brought a thought of something one of the kids had said or done, an image of Mitch's hands touching the wood or the fixtures.

Obviously it was more than the bad memories driving her away: She still had the urge to run.

She finished packing her clothing and personal items, planning to be ready to leave on Saturday morning. She really needed one more day to pull things together.

She should be happier about the offer, and her lack of enthusiasm bothered her. But then, no one had been in a cheerful mood all week. The kids had gone around wearing sullen expressions and Mitch had barely spoken to her.

She felt like the Wicked Witch of the West.

She felt miserable.

By Friday the kitchen was bright and functional, looking nothing like the outdated room it had been only last week. Heather was amazed at the speed of the progress and the beauty of Mitch's woodworking skills. But that day she took the kids into Whitehorn for lunch, needing to get away.

A slim, pale girl with bleached hair sat on one of the booths at the counter, chain smoking and sipping coffee. "Good thing they got that Gavin Nighthawk behind bars," she said to the waitress who filled her cup. "This town wasn't safe with him on the loose."

"I heard that Garrett Kincaid went to visit him in jail and hired him that fancy lawyer, Elizabeth Gardener." The elderly woman who spoke from the first booth was one Heather had noticed every time she'd entered the Hip Hop. Her frizzy hair had the appearance of a dandelion gone to seed, and her gaudy jewelry looked like something the twins would select from the dime store for a Halloween get-up. "They're getting him released on bail."

The young woman at the counter, whom someone called Audra, gave her a hateful glare. "Everyone knows you just sit there all day and make stuff up. Nighthawk is going to prison. Maybe the electric chair."

"All right, ladies," Janie Austin said in censure. "We have customers and some of them are children."

"Thank you," Heather said softly, when Janie came to take their order. Janie leaned down to listen to her speak. "I only know a little about the situation and we're leaving tomorrow, but I think the twins will be living here and I wouldn't want them frightened."

Janie nodded her understanding. "You know," she said, straightening and sliding an order pad out of her pocket, "these are some of the most well-behaved children I've ever waited on. I don't even think Taylor and Ashley are the same girls who came in here at the beginning of summer."

"Oh, it's the same us," Ashley told her with a serious nod. "We just don't act like hooligans no more, least not when we can help it."

Janie laughed in delight. "I think I'd like to treat you all to a free ice cream after you eat your lunch today."

"Aw-right!" the kids chorused.

Heather and Janie laughed at their enthusiasm. Heather couldn't wait to tell Mitch. She ordered a meal to take home for him.

She took the children to the library, where they found a comfortable spot, and she read them the books they brought her until she was hoarse. The librarian smiled pleasantly as they filed out.

"Think we can swim this afternoon?" Patrick asked on the drive home.

"I suppose you can," Heather agreed.

She supervised a couple of hours in the pool, then led them into the house for naps.

She was sitting on the porch with a glass of tea when a battered truck came up the drive and parked on the gravel area. Martin Rollins got out and took his time crossing to the house. "Things sure look in a might better repair around here," he said. He removed his hat, squinted up at the roof and glanced at the outbuildings.

"Come see the kitchen," she offered, and led him into the air-conditioned house.

His faded blue eyes took in the newly remodeled room and he voiced his approval. "I decided on a couple of horses, and I thought I'd better see about the papers. Don't want nobody to think I came by 'em illegally."

She led him into her father's office and opened one of the few files remaining in a desk drawer. "If you can make any sense of these, you're welcome to look. There are bills of sale as well as registration papers."

"We'll need to make this legal," he said.

"I've checked into it," Heather assured him. "I'll have the papers notarized."

After several minutes he selected two sheets of paper. "I have the vet and feed bills here—made a list—so you can see I'm not stealin' from ya."

"I wouldn't think that."

From the pocket of his overalls, he pulled the papers, and a stack of photographs almost fell from his fingers. "I forgot...the missus sent these for you, too."

Heather accepted the black-and-white pictures and studied them. They were photos of a gathering in town, although the buildings looked nothing like those there today. In the center of one picture, her father and mother smiled at the camera.

Heather touched the image of her mother with an index finger. She had only a few photographs of her. "They look so...happy."

"Yep," he replied. "I expect they were. Your pa took it hard when she died. I think he tried hard, for your sake, but I never saw anybody change so much. Seemed like each year he just got crankier and stayed away from people more."

Heather placed the photos on the desktop and hugged herself. "I hated it here."

"Figured that. You never visited him."

"He didn't miss me."

"Seems like he did. He told me about you—about how successful you were in San Francisco."

"He did?" she asked in surprise.

"Showed the missus a Christmas card with a picture of your oldest one year."

"Well, I'll be darned... Well, I never missed being here."

He looked at her oddly, then gathered his papers, and they discussed the final details, as well as how he would handle selling the rest of the stock for her, and she saw him to the door.

"Wish you were stayin'," he said. "You'd make fine neighbors."

She waved him off. The rest of the day her newfound knowledge gave her pause for thought. She hadn't been as insignificant to her father as she'd believed, not if he spoke of her and showed her cards to Mrs. Rollins. Why couldn't he have shown her a little concern or attention while she'd been growing up? Why couldn't he have cared enough to notice how miserable she was? Too little too late. Way too late.

Heather banished the thoughts from her mind and made dinner. She and the kids ate, with lively conversation that helped fill the void left by Mitch's absence from the table. He worked until past dinnertime, then took his meal and left to clean up.

"Mom!" Jessica called to her from the other room as Heather stood trying to figure out the new dishwasher. "Come quick!"

She hurried into the living room. "What?"

"Up here!" Jessica ran up the stairs.

Heather followed her, wondering if this was a true emergency or another one of those kid things.

"There's something in this closet!" She pointed into the closet in the boys's room.

"Like what?"

At the same time she asked, Heather heard pounding coming up the stairs, and the twins were squealing in their most eardrum-piercing pitch.

Mitch appeared in the doorway. "What?"

"In there!" Taylor said. "A mouse or something!"

Mitch stepped past Heather into the near-empty closet.

Heather reached inside and pulled the chain on the light for him. No light came on, and she looked up to see that the light bulb was missing. A little niggle of suspicion clawed at her chest. The light had worked when she'd been packing.

The door closed behind her, blocking out the light,

and a clicking sound met her ears. Children's voices whispered, then disappeared.

"What the—" Mitch bumped into her, then moved away, and she heard him rattling the doorknob. "Taylor! Ashley!"

Stunned for a moment, Heather gathered her thoughts.

"The door's locked," he said.

She tried it herself, as though he wasn't capable of knowing. A shiver of panic traveled up her spine and the stifling darkness closed in around her. She pounded on the door. "Jessica! Jessica!"

Mitch's hands closed over her fingers. "Heather, it's okay."

His hands and his words calmed her enough to strategize her thinking. She wasn't eight years old. She wasn't helpless. She wasn't alone. She took a deep breath. Reason came back. She could handle this. She could handle anything. "Wait."

She moved to the back of the closet and groped on one of the shelves until her fingers came in contact with a dusty box. Opening it, she felt the utility candles and matches. Within seconds, she had a candle lit.

Mitch blinked.

Both of them glanced around.

"I think they did this on purpose," Mitch said.

She rolled his suggestion around. "Jessica?" she asked. "Jessica's never done anything like this."

"Are you suggesting Taylor and Ashley put her up to it?"

"I don't know." She took a minute to look around. "These weren't in here before. I packed the boy's things out of here yesterday." The objects she mentioned were two sleeping bags and a brown sack.

Mitch opened the bag and reached inside, withdrawing a sandwich in a plastic bag. "Smells like peanut butter and jelly."

He actually had half a smile on his face. That got her dander up. "You can't think this is funny!"

"You gotta admit, they must have thought it out."

"But for what purpose?"

"Maybe they want us to talk. We haven't done much of that lately."

She looked away.

"Maybe they want us to think."

Heather pounded on the door again. "Jessica Elizabeth Johnson, you open this door right this minute! If you open it now, I won't punish you. It will just be a joke. If you don't open it right now, you will be in big, big trouble, young lady. I'm going to count to five."

Mitch snickered and she wanted to turn around and hit him.

"One. Two. Three."

Silence.

"Four. Jessica, do you hear me?"

Nothing.

"Five!"

Her mind raced. "Andrew!" she said in near panic. "Where is Andrew?"

"I'm sure he's right there with them."

Heather looked around the inside of the dimly candle-lit closet. She opened the sleeping bags and found two cans of soda and a flashlight. Her heart sank. "How long do they plan to leave us in here? Mitch, break this door down."

"Are you nuts? I've seen how this place is constructed. That door is solid oak." He folded one of the sleeping bags and took a seat. "Might as well get cozy."

Fuming, Heather dripped a little wax on the wood floor well away from them and stuck the candle in it upright. "I'm saving the flashlight batteries."

"A person would think you'd done this before," he said jokingly. "How come you had candles ready? Maybe you planned this."

"I didn't plan this." Insulted, she took a seat, as he had. "I've done this before."

He studied her strangely.

"My father's housekeeper used to lock me in here. Same damned closet." She snorted derisively. "Does life come full circle or what?"

"That's awful," Mitch said, suddenly sober. "That's cruel."

"Yes," she replied. "It was."

"Are you claustrophobic?" he asked, genuine concern etching his brow.

"Not really. I hated it. I hated the darkness at first.

That's when I figured out to hide candles in here. I'm not exactly comfortable, mind you. But I'm not going to go berserk on you.''

''Heather, I'm so sorry. I had no idea.'' He got up and pounded on the door so hard it hurt her ears and she covered them. ''Taylor! Ashley! Open this door or you're never getting ice cream again until you're old ladies with no teeth!''

There was no response from the other side of the door.

Heather held her mouth in a grim line and grappled with her memories.

Mitch sat back down.

A few minutes of silence passed. A soft rustle caught their attention and a piece of paper slid underneath the door toward them.

''Open the door!'' Mitch said sternly.

''Jessica, open this door!'' Heather demanded to no avail.

She reached for the paper. A note was neatly printed in Jessica's ten-year-old penmanship. She read aloud.

''You are scaring Andrew. He's just a baby, so please stop yelling and pounding. We turned up VeggieTales loud, so he can't hear you. We can't hear you neither. We will let you out to-morrow. That should be enough time for you to think about stuff. Please, please, please think more about staying here. Taylor says she will eat peas and carrots. Ashley says she will eat peas and carrots, too, and she won't throw any more tanterms.

"Patrick says he will learn to spell so he can write stuff for you, like the groshery list. I will help you clean and cook.

"Love from your children.

"It's signed by all of them. Except Andrew."
Teary-eyed, Heather passed the note to Mitch.

Twenty-One

Mitch looked over the letter and set it aside.

"I'm sorry, Heather," he said to her.

"You didn't put them up to it, did you?"

"No."

"Well, then, don't be sorry."

A few minutes passed. "Man, Heather. I can't believe what you just told me. You always said that Montana wasn't for you," he said softly. "Is this why? The bad things that happened to you here?"

She took a breath. "I thought so. I was lonely here. My father was an alcoholic, and he ignored me after my mother died. The woman who took care of me was abusive."

"She hit you?"

"Sometimes. Mostly she confined me to my room. If I was really bad, she locked me in here." Heather glanced around. "I hated my father for not stopping her. For not loving me enough to care what happened to me. Maybe he was just too miserable to look beyond his own suffering. Now that I'm an adult, I don't believe he knew she locked me away. But he locked me up in his own way—by shutting me out."

She scooted back against the wall, her anger gone.

"This week I realized that the bad memories are mostly faded away now."

"They must be," he said. "You're handling this."

"This isn't the same house it was then. I'm not the same helpless girl. I'm an adult. I'm in control of my life. And I make choices for myself and my children."

"That's pretty sane thinking."

"Yeah, well, I've spent quite a few hours in counseling. That's what helped me make the break from my husband."

"You talked about freedom before, and I think I understand now. You wanted to be free of this place and the memories."

"Yes, but I did it foolishly. I latched on to someone I believed was strong, and I thought of him as my savior. I knew he had drive and that he would succeed somewhere better, and I wanted to go.

"He did have drive and ambition, and he did succeed in the things he planned. But he drove me, too. He created the successful partner he needed, and I went along, being manipulated."

"You must have realized what was happening. That you weren't happy."

"I always knew I was unhappy with him. After I was treated for depression, I started facing why. And then I found out I was pregnant with Andrew, and it all seemed so helpless. I finally got the help I needed and made the decisions I needed to make. I won't ever go back to that way of life again."

The candlelight flickered. "Not all husbands are like he was," Mitch pointed out.

"But you don't know," she said. "You just don't know until it's too late. And I couldn't go through that again."

"And that's why you wouldn't give us a chance?"

She nodded.

"Because you're afraid."

She met his gaze warily.

"What is it you're afraid of?" he asked.

The truth washed over her in a wave. "That horrible feeling of being out of control. Giving up myself."

"Sometimes you just have to trust."

"That horrible realization that you've made a terrible mistake and you can't take it back," she continued.

Mitch studied her expression. He scooted forward and took her hand. "It's not me you don't trust, is it? It's yourself."

Tears burned behind her eyes. "I couldn't stand to fail again," she said hoarsely. "And I'm afraid to trust myself to make such an important decision."

"You said it, Heather," he said softly, and stroked her cheek. "You're not a child any longer. You're old enough to know what you want and choose wisely. You're not helpless. You're in control."

"There is no control over things like that," she disagreed. "That was a ten-year section of my life wasted."

"I think those kids of yours are something pretty great that came of it."

She hung her head and whispered, "Yes. Thank goodness, yes."

Mitch moved closer yet, spread one hand over her bare knee. "Sometimes you have to trust your heart," he said. "There's nothing I can give you that you don't have already, so that's not why you would choose me."

"You're wrong. You couldn't be more wrong."

"Why?"

"You're *everything* I've never had before. Maybe I'd make a choice because of the way you make me feel or—" she looked away sharply "—or the way you make love to me."

"Those are good things, listen to yourself."

"But are they right for me?" Slowly she allowed her gaze to come back to his earnest one.

"What does your heart tell you?" he asked.

"Is it my heart? Or is it this woman's body that's been deprived for so long?"

"You're so hard on yourself," he said with a smile. "You can love me without needing me. You can want me and not sign your soul over to me. I wouldn't want you like that. Physical need is different from complete dependence on another person. But I know something about myself that I believe is true about you, too."

"What's that?"

"There's no separating sex and love. That's why

it's called lovemaking. A physical relationship gets the heart involved.''

"I never loved my husband."

"Do you love me?"

Her heart stopped.

His question hung in the air between them, dancing like kinetic energy she could feel along her skin, at the roots of her hair.

Her heart started again, and the answer was there in the frantic beating. *Yes.* The word frightened her. The fact frightened her more. How vulnerable she would be to a man she truly loved. It wasn't just staying in Montana. It wasn't just leaving her job. It was losing herself that frightened her.

"You're stronger than you think you are," he said. "You proved that when you were eight years old and put those candles in here."

She glanced at the flame and considered his words.

"You got yourself out of this place, even if you made some sacrifices to do it. But you ended up getting yourself out of that situation, too. You've been in control."

It hadn't seemed like control.

"If you do love me," he said, "will you ever be truly happy if you don't acknowledge it? Does it keep you safe if you lock up love and don't tell anyone, don't admit it?"

"You loved your wife," she said. "And look where it got you."

"Where?" he asked.

"Hurt."

He picked up her hand and studied her fingers. "Of course I hurt when she was sick. And I hurt when she died. Because I loved her. But I wouldn't change loving her, or having what we had together, in order to have never hurt."

He traced a finger one by one over hers, around her wrist. A wry smile turned up his lips. "I'm a fine one to be telling you this."

"Why?"

"Because I've spent the past couple of weeks working at not loving you so that I wouldn't be hurt again." He chuckled. "It hasn't worked. So, if you're going to leave, I might as well love you all I can while you're here. If I'm going to hurt later, I want to enjoy now."

His sincerity touched her. His words amazed her. His touch on her hand set her skin atingle. When he looked up and leaned toward her, Heather had already moved into the kiss she anticipated. Their lips met in a questing, eager blend of warm velvety skin and moist breath.

Would she ever be happy if she didn't acknowledge her feelings for him? Was he right? Were want and need two different things?

She took her hand from his to place it behind his neck and preserve the enticing contact. It wasn't just this. She'd been wrong to question her feelings as only physical desire. This was simply the crowning pleasure of what her heart wanted to express. She could choose to love him.

His arms went around her, and hers found their way to his back, and they clung that way, suspended in time and place. Mitch flipped the sleeping bag open and pulled her down beside him. Their kisses grew feverish and impatient. He covered her breast through her T-shirt and kneaded.

Through her fog of desire, she had sense to ask, "Mitch, what if the kids open the door?"

He cursed softly. Then he stood and pulled his belt out of his belt loops. "You have a belt on?"

She shook her head.

"Give me your bra."

She pulled her arms inside her shirt, unhooked her bra and handed it to him. He fastened it to his belt, secured the belt end to the doorknob and the silk lingerie end to the rod above their heads.

Heather laughed out loud. "Were you a MacGyver fan?"

He chuckled and pulled off his T-shirt.

The smile left her face.

He joined her on the sleeping bag. "Let me help you off with this."

"And these?"

"Especially those."

"Now yours...I've been watching these muscles all week, wanting to touch them."

"Let's not waste any more time. Don't fold my jeans, for crying out loud. Was that a giggle?"

"I love it when you kiss me there."

"What about here?"

"Ah. Especially there."

"Your skin's so soft...all over. I like you in candlelight."

"There's so much I love about you, Mitch. Hurry."

"Now?"

"Yes. Mmm...yes...I don't think...I could bear...to leave you."

"Don't."

Sometime later, dressed in his jeans, Mitch glanced at his watch. "Suppose they're all asleep?"

"Probably." She snuggled against his bare chest.

He loved the feeling, but his stomach was ready to growl. "I'm getting hungry." He sat and opened the sack. Handing her a bagged sandwich, he asked, "Want to share a cola?"

"No, thanks."

"You sure?"

"Sure I don't want to have to go to the bathroom."

"Oh, yeah." He hadn't even thought about that. Yet.

They munched sandwiches, touched each other's faces and hands, and shared smiles.

"Mitch?"

"Hmm?"

"What about Trina?"

"We mutually decided we weren't cut out for each other."

"Really? She's awfully pretty. And young. And firm."

"I'd rather eat peanut butter in a closet with you than filet mignon in the best restaurant in the state with her. Firm or no firm. I'd rather share a—" he glanced down "—Barbie sleeping bag with you than a deluxe cabin on a cruise liner with her."

"You would?"

"I would." He drew an X over his heart.

"You sure know how to lay it on thick."

"Yeah."

She kissed his peanut butter-flavored lips. "Mitch?"

"Yeah?"

"I love you."

His cocky smile faltered. He had difficulty swallowing the bite he'd just taken. He set his crust aside and took hers from her. "I love you, too, Heather."

She gazed into his incredible, sincere golden-brown eyes, loving him more every minute, *choosing* to love him more every minute.

"Will you marry me?" he asked.

Her heart jumped. But it wasn't out of fear this time. It was out of love—and happiness. The only thing she truly had to let go of was her fear. "Yes."

He kissed her and they laughed, at the peanut butter and the bizarre location.

"What does this mean?" he asked, his expression growing serious. "What about your job in San Francisco?"

"They're managing fine without me."

"You'd leave it? What about your career?"

"I'd like to explore being a wife and a mother for a while—until I decide what it is I'd like to do. I own some good horses. I'm sure there's a thriving business there somewhere. I can make my own choices now. Can't I?"

"Here?" he asked. "In Montana?"

"Do you think if we slip a note back out under the door, telling them we'll stay, they'll let us use the bathroom?"

"The question is—will they let us back in?"

The punishment for locking people in a closet as yet undetermined, the children spent the morning wavering from trepidation to triumphant joy.

"You're really going to get married?" Taylor asked for the tenth time as they sat around the table in the new kitchen.

"And we really get to stay *here?*" Jess inquired.

"I've turned down the offer for the sale of the ranch," Heather replied.

"Yeah, I heard that." Mitch started a pot of coffee.

"How did you hear?" She hadn't told him.

"My agent called to say you'd turned down my offer. I thought it was pretty generous, too."

"*Your* offer!" She stared at him. "You made that bid?"

"Yup. I pulled a few strings and was ready to sell

some stocks, as well as get a loan. This place doesn't come cheap.''

"You were going to buy it?''

He nodded. "Seems like home to me now.''

He stepped toward her and she hugged him. "To me, too.''

"Are you guys gonna hug all the time?'' Ashley asked.

"Yes,'' her father replied. "And kiss, too.''

He kissed Heather, and around the table the children giggled.

"What do you guys want for lunch?'' Heather asked, changing the subject.

"Skettios!'' Taylor shouted.

"I'm really craving peanut butter,'' Mitch drawled, and nuzzled her cheek.

She pushed him away playfully, and he seated himself beside Patrick.

"Does this mean we get to keep the horses?'' Jess asked.

"Oh! The horses!'' Heather sprinted to the phone. "I have to call Martin and tell him to stop the auction.''

Jess grinned at Mitch.

Andrew pitched a fit in his chair, and Mitch took him out and held him on his lap.

The ranch was nearly workable and the renovated house had evolved into a home they'd created together—no longer the house of Heather's childhood.

New memories and once-impossible dreams had replaced the past.

"We need to give the ranch a new name," Mitch said when Heather returned from her call.

Jessica had been doodling on a pad of paper, and her well-drawn circle gave him an idea. He took a red crayon and made a number seven inside it.

"Circle Seven?" Heather asked. "I like it."

Mitch observed the circle of smiling faces around the table. "Me, too."

"Me, too," Taylor said. "Now can we please have skettios?"

Mitch met Heather's shimmering eyes, seeing her happiness and knowing, without a doubt, that this woman was what his life had been missing. No matter what the future held—and it would hold plenty if these children were any indication—they could weather it together.

* * * * *

MONTANA MAVERICKS:
WED IN WHITEHORN

continues next month with

OUTLAW MARRIAGE
by Laurie Paige
Turn the page for an exciting preview...

tered pickup, the standard mode of transportation to
about ninety percent of the rural residents of Montana.

One

Hope Baxter exhaled a pensive sigh, her gaze on the mountains to the west of Whitehorn. Today the lofty peaks didn't comfort her troubled spirit. Neither did they gain her any perspective on the problems confronting her.

Not that the problems were personal, she hastened to assure herself.

The elaborately hand-carved sign on the lawn that proclaimed the building to be the new headquarters of the Baxter Development Corporation reminded her of her duties. She squared her shoulders and glanced toward the neatly arranged papers on her desk.

As the chief attorney on the case of *Baxter versus Kincaid, et al,* she had to be cool, decisive and firm in the meeting with Collin Kincaid. She wondered where he was. Punctual in their prior meetings, he was ten minutes late for this one and he was the one who had requested it.

A movement caught her eye. She paused, her attention on the street in front of the building, and watched as a tall, agile rancher climbed out of a battered pickup, the standard mode of transportation for about ninety percent of the rural residents of Montana.

He walked up the sidewalk toward the entrance of the building.

Collin Kincaid. Handsome as all the Kincaid men were. Eyes like blue sapphires. Dark, almost-black, hair. Half a foot taller than her own five-seven stature, giving him the height advantage even when she wore high heels. He was also muscular. His palm had been callused when they had shaken hands at their first meeting. He was a working rancher, not an armchair cowboy.

Collin was also the only legitimate grandson of Garrett Kincaid. Garrett was trying to buy the old Kincaid spread from the trustees who managed the ranch for seven-year-old Jenny McCallum, the heir to the throne, so to speak. The grandfather wanted to provide a legacy for the other six grandsons—a seventh hadn't been found yet but was thought to exist— all of whom were the bastard offspring of Garrett's deceased son, Larry Kincaid.

Oh, what tangled webs we weave...

Not just Larry with his profligate womanizing, she mused, but all humans. She gave a snort of amusement. My, but she was waxing philosophical today.

Because Collin Kincaid made her nervous? Because she'd felt the unmistakable pull of male-female interest between them the first time they'd met? Because they were enemies?

Impatient with her thoughts, she resumed her seat in the executive chair and pulled herself up closer to the desk. It was an effective shield, she'd found, for dealing with those who didn't take her seriously as an attorney.

The secretary buzzed her on the intercom and announced Kincaid's arrival.

"Send him in," she requested. She didn't stand when the door opened. Keeping her seat kept her in the position of authority. In this office, she was the one in charge.

His eyes crinkled at the corners when he smiled upon seeing her. Their startling blue depths held laughter as he advanced across the Oriental carpet, as if he knew more than he was telling. And saw more than she was willing to reveal.

He was dressed in a gray summer suit with a touch of blue in the weave. His shirt was white and immaculate, his tie a tasteful blend of blue and gray with a touch of red.

Understated. Nothing too obvious, yet he had an aura of power that could have been intimidating had a person less confidence in his or her own abilities.

She returned his smile with cool professionalism.

He had a way of acting older and more experienced in the ways of the world than she, but that was ridiculous. He was only thirty-one to her almost twenty-eight. She'd gone to college at one of the prestigious Ivy League schools back east while he'd attended a Montana university. She'd been raised in New York until her father had decided to move back to Whitehorn a few years ago. Collin had lived most of his life on a ranch. Except for a few years with his mom and stepfather in San Diego after his parents divorced.

She wondered if that had been a lonely time for him. He'd returned to his grandfather's ranch over in Elk Springs when he was fourteen or thereabouts, so the town gossips had reported. He'd been a rebel at the time, but hard work and a firm hand from his grandfather had soon put him to rights, the local story went.

Not that Hope cared in the least about Collin's past, but knowledge of one's enemy was a good thing. She cleared her throat and nodded firmly.

"Good morning. Please be seated," she invited briskly, gesturing to the guest chair at the opposite side of the desk. Her tone was crisp, decisive.

He casually pulled the chair to the side of the desk, angling it toward her, then sat and stretched out his long legs so that his black dress boots were within two feet of her chair.

This action encroached on her space and forced her to angle her chair sideways to face him in a full frontal position, which she favored as one of greater power. It also put her feet within touching range of his, which further decreased the autonomy of her position.

"So," he said in his deep, pleasant baritone, "we meet again."

There was a world of innuendo in the statement. As if they'd been lovers or something in the not-too-distant past.

"Yes," she said coolly, and picked up the Kincaid file. She flipped it open and studied the first page without really seeing it. Realizing she was using the folder as a shield, she tossed it back onto the desk, disgusted with her cowardice. "I don't see that we have anything more to discuss," she said, deftly reminding him that he had been the one to request the meeting.

"Don't you?" he inquired with lazy humor.

He laid his creamy white Stetson hat, which he'd been holding, on her credenza. She was chagrined with herself for not telling him to hang it on the antique lowboy beside her door. Now he was further ensconced in her space.

In fact, she was beginning to feel surrounded by his confident masculinity. His eyes, as blue as the Montana sky, studied her. There was nothing lazy or humorous in that probing perusal. Her heart beat faster as she shifted uneasily in the executive chair.

Annoyed, she told him, "Past meetings between our parties have not been productive."

"Well," he drawled in that maddening Western accent, "your dad and my grandfather tend to get a mite heated on the subject. I thought you and I could discuss a possible settlement more fully without them being present."

His eyes raked over her navy-blue coat dress that fastened all the way down the front with red-and-white enameled buttons. He lingered at the last button, which was located four inches above the hemline. Her knee was visible in the slit thus created.

Hope pulled her chair close to the desk so that her legs were hidden and twisted sideways from the waist so she could face him. "Does this mean you're accepting our terms for settling the case?"

He had the nerve to laugh. The crinkles appeared beside his eyes again and twin lines indented his lean cheeks. His teeth were very white in contrast to his tanned face. His lips curved alluringly at the corners. She stared at his mouth and wondered about his kiss, how it would feel, if his lips would be hard or tender as he touched hers—

Appalled, she broke the thought.

He was the enemy. She had to remember that....

Silhouette
bestselling authors

KASEY MICHAELS

RUTH LANGAN

CAROLYN ZANE

welcome you to a world of family, privilege and power with three brand-new love stories about America's most beloved dynasty, the Coltons

Brides of Privilege

Available May 2001

Silhouette®

Where love comes alive™

Visit Silhouette at www.eHarlequin.com
PSCOLT

REGENCY
ROMANCE

Visit the elegant English countryside,
explore the whirlwind of London Society
and meet feisty heroines who tame roguish
heroes with their wit, zest and feminine
charm, in...The Regency Collection.

Available in March 2001 at your favorite retail outlet:

TRUE COLOURS
by Nicola Cornick

THE WOLFE'S MATE
by Paula Marshall

MR. TRELAWNEY'S
PROPOSAL
by Mary Brendan

TALLIE'S KNIGHT
by Anne Gracie

Visit us at www.eHarlequin.com

RCREG2

PRESCRIPTION ROMANCE

Get swept away by
these warmhearted romances featuring
dedicated doctors and nurses....

LOVE IS JUST
A HEARTBEAT AWAY!

Available in April 2001 at your favorite retail outlet:

HOLDING THE BABY
by Laura MacDonald

TENDER LIAISON
by Joanna Neil

A FAMILIAR FEELING
by Margaret Barker

HEAVEN SENT
by Carol Wood

Visit us at www.eHarlequin.com

RCPRE2

Silhouette® —

where love comes alive—online...

eHARLEQUIN.com

shop eHarlequin

- ♥ Find all the new Silhouette releases at everyday great discounts.

- ♥ Try before you buy! Read an excerpt from the latest Silhouette novels.

- ♥ Write an online review and share your thoughts with others.

reading room

- ♥ Read our Internet exclusive daily and weekly online serials, or vote in our interactive novel.

- ♥ Talk to other readers about your favorite novels in our Reading Groups.

- ♥ Take our Choose-a-Book quiz to find the series that matches you!

authors' alcove

- ♥ Find out interesting tidbits and details about your favorite authors' lives, interests and writing habits.

- ♥ Ever dreamed of being an author? Enter our Writing Round Robin. The Winning Chapter will be published online! Or review our writing guidelines for submitting your novel.

All this and more available at
www.eHarlequin.com
on Women.com Networks

SINTB1R

LONG, TALL TEXANS

EMMETT, REGAN & BURKE

New York Times
extended list bestselling author

Diana PALMER

returns to Jacobsville, Texas, in this special
collection featuring rugged heroes, spirited
heroines and passionate love stories told
in her own inimitable way!

Coming in May 2001 only from Silhouette Books!

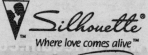

Silhouette®
Where love comes alive™

Visit Silhouette at www.eHarlequin.com

PSLLT

Finding Home

New York Times bestselling authors

Linda Howard
Elizabeth Lowell
Kasey Michaels

invite you on
the journey of a lifetime.

Three women are searching—
each wants a place to belong,
a man to care for her,
a child to love.

Will her wishes be fulfilled?

*Coming in April 2001
only from Silhouette Books!*

Silhouette®

Where love comes alive™

Visit Silhouette at www.eHarlequin.com   PSHOME

Every mother wants to see her children marry and have little ones of their own.

One mother decided to take matters into her own hands....

Now three Texas-born brothers are about to discover that mother knows best: A strong man *does* need a good woman. And babies make a forever family!

Matters of the Heart

A Mother's Day collection of three **brand-new** stories by

Pamela Morsi
Ann Major
Annette Broadrick

Available in April at your favorite retail outlets, only from Silhouette Books!

Where love comes alive™

Visit Silhouette at www.eHarlequin.com   PSMOTH

WED IN WHITEHORN...
where legends live on
and love lasts forever!

If you missed any of the first nine books in the
MONTANA MAVERICKS series, here's
a chance to order your copy today!

MONTANA MAVERICKS

#65046	**LONE STALLION'S LADY** by Lisa Jackson	$4.50 U.S.☐ $5.25 CAN.☐
#65047	**CHEYENNE BRIDE** by Laurie Paige	$4.50 U.S.☐ $5.25 CAN.☐
#65048	**YOU BELONG TO ME** by Jennifer Greene	$4.50 U.S.☐ $5.25 CAN.☐
#65049	**THE MARRIAGE BARGAIN** by Victoria Pade	$4.50 U.S.☐ $5.25 CAN.☐
#65050	**BIG SKY LAWMAN** by Marilyn Pappano	$4.50 U.S.☐ $5.25 CAN.☐
#65051	**THE BABY QUEST** by Pat Warren	$4.50 U.S.☐ $5.25 CAN.☐
#65052	**IT HAPPENED ONE WEDDING NIGHT** by Karen Hughes	$4.50 U.S.☐ $5.25 CAN.☐
#65053	**THE BIRTH MOTHER** by Pamela Toth	$4.50 U.S.☐ $5.25 CAN.☐
#65054	**RICH, RUGGED...RUTHLESS** by Jennifer Mikels	$4.50 U.S.☐ $5.25 CAN.☐

(limited quantities available)

TOTAL AMOUNT	$
POSTAGE & HANDLING	$
($1.00 for one book, 50¢ for each additional)	
APPLICABLE TAXES*	$ _____
TOTAL PAYABLE	$ _____
(check or money order—please do not send cash)	

To order, send the completed form, along with a check or money order for the total above, payable to Montana Mavericks, to: **In the U.S.:** 3010 Walden Avenue, P.O. Box 9077, Buffalo, NY 14269-9077 **In Canada:** P.O. Box 636, Fort Erie, Ontario L2A 5X3.

Name: _____

Address: _____ City: _____

State/Prov.: _____ Zip/Postal Code: _____

Account # (if applicable): _____ 075 CSAS

*New York residents remit applicable sales taxes.
Canadian residents remit applicable
GST and provincial taxes.

Silhouette®

Visit Silhouette at www.eHarlequin.com   MONMAVBACK9